HOWARD G BLAIR

SNIPER WITH A VENGEANCE

D1738912

CHAPTER ONE

The shooter figured the shot was a very difficult one. The target had to be located within one hundred yards of where the rifle scope had been focused. The target would be moving from right to left between 65 miles per hour, which meant the shooter had to locate the target and get ready and shoot in less than five seconds. The shooter knew the approximate time the target would be driving by, and the car the target was using. The problem facing the shooter was the possibility that a large eighteen-wheel truck may shield the target when the time came to shoot.

The shooter knew the target. A week ago, the target, Mr. Cooper, was in competition with the shooter's friend. Both were trying to sell two large earthmovers to a well-known Albuquerque contractor. The shooter learned that Mr. Cooper got the deal, and the friend was devastated. *Well, I guess I know my target,* thought the shooter. In the next four days the shooter followed the target where Mr. Cooper worked, where he lived, what time he drove home, and the route he took. The shooter took a place behind a midsized rock located on a rocky hill overlooking Interstate 40 that Mr. Cooper took on his way home.

The shooter waited and watched for Cooper's car. When it was spotted, the shooter quickly put an eye to the rifle scope, stopped breathing for a moment, saw the target come into the scope area, and pulled the trigger.

* * *

Fred Cooper was in a good mood as he drove west on highway 40 toward Edgewood. He was a medium sized man of five feet ten inches tall. He tried to keep in good shape but the entertaining he had to do with customers gave him twenty pounds over what he wanted to weigh. His stomach was not protruding too much but was starting to bother him. Two days ago, he had just finished selling two earthmovers to a major contractor in Albuquerque, a project he had been working on for three weeks. The deal had been agreed upon, but it took two days for the paperwork to be finalized and signed. Fred knew that anything could happen in those two days and was relieved everything went smoothly. The action that made him feel so good was the fact that he beat the great competitor Caterpillar. He knew the main reason he got the order was because of price, but it didn't matter, he got the order. He called his wife knowing she was going to be incredibly happy with the commission.

"What is it, Fred?" his wife June answered.

"I got the paperwork signed. There was one sticky detail left but I worked it out."

June's mood lightened, "So, what did you do to get him to sign on the bottom line?"

"Well, the last point was that Caterpillar has a program that if the customer orders an important part for their machine and the part is not available in twelve hours, the part is free."

"Really, how can they do that?"

"June, I've told you they have an extensive parts system so they can make those kinds of guarantees. We don't have anything like that."

"So, what did you do?"

"I discussed the problem with Russell, our general manager and we produced the idea of guaranteeing a free replacement machine within twenty-four hours if the contractor's machine goes down and we can't get it fixed. The replacement unit will stay on his job until we can get his unit running again. That did the trick."

He was smiling to himself when the car window behind him suddenly shattered, and he heard a THUMP on the opposite rear door. At first, he had no idea what happened, and it scared the hell out of him. He struggled to keep control of the car and looked for a place to pull over. In the next few seconds, he got control of his breathing and found a side spot in the road and stopped the car.

June was still on the phone, "What was that?"

"I'll call you back as soon as I can."

"Are you OK?"

"Yes. I'm fine. We'll talk later."

He carefully exited the car and stood looking at the shattered window. He discovered a vast majority of the glass was inside the car in little pieces. He also noted a hole in the rear door.

It took Fred a few seconds to deduce that someone had shot at him as he was driving down the freeway. He instinctively looked around at the rocky hills that were across the road on the driver's side, knowing there would be no one there because he went a quarter mile down the road after the shot before he pulled off the road. He called 911, explained the problem and got back in his car to wait for a police officer to drive up. He called his wife once again and tried to stop shaking.

The State Police car rolled up a half hour later and agreed with Fred's deduction.

"I didn't think a bullet would shatter glass like that?" relayed Fred.

"Cars today use laminated glass for the back windows and generally for the windshield," responded the officer. "Laminated glass will break into a thousand little pieces for safety reasons. It is also easier to clean up."

The officer examined the rear passenger door and found where the bullet went through the door. Both Fred and the officer knew it was almost impossible to find the bullet to determine the caliber used by the shooter.

The officer looked at Cooper and said, "Do you know anyone who would do this? Anyone you pissed off lately?"

Cooper thought for a moment and said, "No Sir. I have no idea who would want to shoot me. Maybe it was just some kid or person shooting at any car that came by."

"Maybe. The bullet hole is distorted due to the angle of the trajectory," said the officer. "The bullet came in at a downward angle due to the hill, and the exit hole is oblong, plus you don't know exactly where you were along I-forty when the bullet struck. I'm afraid all you are going to get from this experience is a police report."

"How are you going to find out who did this?"

"He will strike again, somewhere in New Mexico. They'll keep shooting until they make a mistake. Eventually, we'll get them. Only problem is we don't know how many people will die before we stop his madness."

CHAPTER TWO

Wilt Morrison was sitting in his office reading the Albuquerque Journal when he came across a small story about someone shooting at a driver going east on Interstate 40. Wilt remembered his days as a sniper in the U. S. Marine Corps. Part of his training was to analyze certain types of situations that occurred. He put the paper down, closed his eyes, and thought, *going east on I-40 means the shooter would be in the hills on the south side of the road. The traffic going west toward Albuquerque would be between the shooter and his target. There are numerous trucks on that road going toward and away from Albuquerque. The shooter would have to locate a target between trucks going both ways, quickly estimate the speed of the target and take his shot only viewing the target for less than a second. An impossible shot. I'm surprised the bullet even hit the car, much less the window close to the driver. One thing for sure is the target was random because there is no way you could plan a hit on a specific target on that hill with that traffic. The shooter knew that also. The shooter also knew if he missed and the bullet went through the car, it depended if the target was in the inside lane, or outside land where the bullet would end up. If the target were passing a truck the bullet would be somewhere going down the road with the eighteen-wheeler. If the road were clear, the bullet would be either embedded in the asphalt or skipping down the road for a while. In either case it would never be found. Based on everything I'm thinking about, I'm sure it's a want-to-be-sniper.*

Wilt's thoughts were interrupted when his phone rang. He hesitated before pushing the ANSWER display, gathered his thoughts, put the phone to his ear and said, "Hi Georgie." Wilt had met Georgianna Frost because he was thinking of taking the case of the murder of Jack Frost, a fellow private investigator. Georgianna, or Georgie, took to Wilt and helped him with her former husband's case.

* * *

It has been six months since Pearl Henderson was killed. Wilt missed her much more than he thought he would because she was his confidant and his lover. He found himself turning over in bed at night automatically reaching for her and being surprised for a moment when she wasn't there. He looked forward to coming home after work and sitting down with Pearl and having a glass of wine. It was an empty feeling when he remembered she was gone. Many times, when something came up he thought *I must tell Pearl tonight,* but remembered, she was killed. He found himself tearing up sometimes when he talked about her. When that happened, he had to stop talking because he couldn't get the words out. *Damn Pearl, I miss you so much. If I can form an image in my mind, she's not gone.* He thought about how she saved his life from dying from alcohol poisoning when he got depressed in San Francisco a few years back. *Rest in peace, my love, I owe you and I will try and not shame your name or your reputation.*

After Pearl was laid to rest, Georgie Frost helped Wilt get through the emotional trauma of getting rid of Pearl's things and helping to collect any death benefits. Georgie also worked the garage sale on Pearl's clothes. Wilt didn't know any of Pearl's family and didn't think there were any. Pearl never talked about family except that her parents had died a few years back, and she and her first husband didn't have any children. In fact, Wilt had never met Pearl's former husband and she indicated they didn't have a cordial relationship.

A month after Pearl's things were disposed of Georgie asked Wilt if he wanted to move in with her. Wilt thought it was too soon to decide to commit and expressed the same to Georgie. She accepted his feelings but kept being his friend and asked him over for dinner once a week.

"Hi Honey. I'd like you to come to dinner tonight because Jack Jr. will be home and even though you have met him, I don't think you really know him."

Jack Jr. was a sophomore at the University of New Mexico in Albuquerque and was studying for his degree in history. He and Wilt met at Pearl's funeral and Wilt thought Jack Jr. was ignoring him because Georgie kept hanging on to him. *This would be a chance to find out our feelings about this relationship.*

"That would be fine with me. I'll be finished here in a couple of hours so how does five o'clock sound."

"See you at five, sweety."

Wilt clicked the phone off and stood there thinking. *Georgie is really a sweet woman. She's cute, funny, has a nice body and is aggressive about touching and sex. Yet, there is something about her that makes me uncomfortable at times. At parties I'm waiting for her to embarrass me and I'm not at ease in social gatherings. Georgie helped me after Pearl's death and made going through the grieving process easier. I owe her a lot, but I'm not ready to move in with her because I know how difficult it would be if sometime in the future I wanted to move out.*

* * *

Georgie answered the door and gave Wilt a hug and a kiss on the lips. She put her arm around his and pressed her breasts against him as she walked him into the dining room. Jack Jr. was standing in the middle of the room with a drink in his hand.

I wonder if Jack notices where Georgie's breast is. Wilt put on a smile, ejected himself from Georgie and walked over to Jack Jr. "Hello Jack. Nice to see you again." He started for the bar to fix himself a drink.

"How's the private investigator business?" asked Jack.

"There is always someone who wants to know something about someone and are willing to pay to find out. Once they find out they are pissed at the investigator for finding it out."

Jack Jr. laughed. His laugh broke what little tension was in the room.

"You are majoring in History, is that right?"

"Yes, it's the only thing I find of interest at this time."

"What can you do with a four-year degree in History?"

"Really, not much. You need to go on and get a PhD if you want to teach in a college or university. I'm not sure I want to do that." Jack Jr. was silent a moment, "What's it take to be a sniper in the Marine Corps?"

Wilt was surprised at the question and hesitated. "The short answer is to first go through boot camp, get in the infantry and work to get promoted to at least a Lance Corporal. You must be chosen for Advanced Infantry and Marksman Technique school. Once you complete the AIMT school the next thing is Special Operations School. You end up going through the Scout/Sniper Training Manual. This is all predicated on the fact that you can hit the target, which may be as much as five thousand yards away. Training lasts for seventy-nine days.

"Would it help if I graduated from college first?"

"It might. But if you have a degree and want to go into the Marine Corps, go to Officers Training School and get your bars rather than go in as a private."

"Could I go to sniper's school?"

"No, officers cannot be snipers. They need to control the platoon or whatever their command is."

Georgie interrupted their conversation, "Gentlemen, we are ready to sit down for dinner. Enough of this Marine Corps talk. Jack, if you want to go in the military join the Air Force like your father did."

Dinner went well and dessert was excellent. As they were completing the last bites, Georgie asked Wilt, "Do you want to spend the night Wilt darling?"

Wilt felt himself turning red and did not look at Jack Jr. "Thanks Georgie, but I must get up early tomorrow as I'm going to visit the Albuquerque Police Department to see if they need help catching the this Sniper that is shooting people around New Mexico." *I don't know where that idea came from, but it could be a darn good one.*

After dinner Wilt and Jack Jr. went their separate ways from the driveway. In five minutes, Wilt turned around and went back to Georgie's.

"I knew you'd come back," she said as she opened the door.

"I don't know why you work to embarrass me." Wilt said as Georgie was unbuttoning his shirt."

"Because you're cute when you get red," she said as she kissed him.

"There's got to be an easier way," Wilt mumbled as she led him into the bedroom.

CHAPTER THREE

The shooter was having trouble lying still. She was soaked with sweat and thought she could feel small bugs crawling on her skin trying to get some moisture. *That shot on the I-40 eastbound was a big screw-up. I knew it was going to be difficult, but I didn't think it through. Not enough time to find the target, mentally calculate the lead, and fire. Plus climbing up that rocky hill at night and waiting until the next night to leave was a pain in the ass. At least I'm sure no one saw me. This shot will be easier.*

Helcom Garcia was twenty-four years old. She was a little below five feet six but made up for the height problem by weighing almost two hundred pounds. She did everything in excess to prove she was better than most men. Growing up in New Mexico, she learned to shoot from Uncle Rod, who was an avid hunter. Garcia's father wanted a son when Helcom was born, thus the name, "Hell, here comes another girl." She grew up with four sisters. Her father never paid any attention to her, and she knew he wanted a son, not a fifth daughter. Her mother was always busy with the house and her sisters. Helcom decided since her father wanted a son, she would do what she could to be the male in the family. She played rough, joined boy's games, and was the quintessential Tom Boy. Her father died of a heart attack when she was ten years old. That didn't stop Helcom from continuing to strive to master male activities. Her father's life insurance left enough for the family to have a nice nest egg for a few years. When she was eighteen she got a job at the local shooting range. Her responsibility was to check shooters in and out of the range. The job was just what she wanted because she only worked four days a week for three weeks and had the fourth week off. She also received a discount on the ammunition, so practice shooting didn't cost her very much.

Helcom idealized her uncle Rod and wanted to be a Marine like Rod. "Once a Marine, always a Marine," Uncle Rod would say. Helcom figured she would be a sniper because she was a good shot and loved the feel of a rifle against her shoulder. When she was eighteen, she thought about enlisting, but because of her weight she had doubts about being turned down by the military. She called the Army recruiter and told him she had a son and gave him his height and weight. The recruiter said that her son needed to lose at least fifty pounds before he would be considered a viable recruit. He explained that the Marine Corps, Air Force, and the Coast Guard, would have the same requirement. Helcom also asked if women could be snipers in the Army? The recruiter told her there were no female snipers in any of the branches of the armed services. Helcom hung up the phone extremely disappointed. *I'll show these bastards that I can be a sniper and they are making a big mistake not taking me.*

With the remaining insurance money from her father, Helcom had saved up enough money to purchase a high-end sniper rifle. The Ruger American Rifle, model 6903, .308 caliber was an excellent weapon for her work. It has a lightweight stock, held four cartridges, and offered options like a tripod at the end of the barrel, which she added to the package. She also bought a Bushnell Elite Tactical G2DMR scope that offered 6 to 24 magnifications, which was currently set at twelve power.

She gave a lot of thought about shooting at people in and around New Mexico. She thought there should be a purpose in who was her target. *Some person that did something bad to another person or a friend. That bad person was destined to die from one of my bullets.* Her job at the shooting range gave her the opportunity to meet and listen to lots of talk between those checking in and out of the range. A week ago, one of the Trap shooters was telling his friend about the affair he was having with his secretary. He acted proud that his wife had no idea what he was doing. He was a good-looking middle-aged man who dressed well. Helcom noticed the wedding ring on his finger and the diamond ring on his right hand. He also had a Rolex watch on his left wrist.

His poor wife is home waiting for her husband and he's running around with some floozy from his office. He doesn't deserve to live.

Helcom followed the braggart outside and wrote down the model and color of his pickup and the number on his license plate and noticed the LOBO sign on the front of the vehicle. She followed him home a couple of times. She learned by listing at the shooting range that next Tuesday he was going to drive to Grants going westbound on I-40. He said he was leaving around four in the afternoon. When she returned home she spent an hour figuring the estimated time he would pass a certain portion of the road that was straight for a half mile.

* * *

She heard the cars coming around the curves before they entered the straight away. She had picked a spot-on top of a hill looking down on Interstate 40 going west. The hill was covered with scrub brush, and she was hidden between the brush and the loose dirt around the hill. The view of the west bound traffic was excellent as there was a long stretch of straight road coming toward the hill. Helcom could pick any car or truck she wanted but she was waiting for a red pick-up with LOBO as the front license plate.

People buy red cars because they want to be noticed. Well, they're going to be noticed this morning. I just need to estimate the speed of the car and aim accordingly.

There were three vehicles coming toward her: two cars and one pickup. All three were passing a sixteen wheeled truck and were close together. The first car in line was a red pick-up. Helcom noticed the LOBO on the front of the truck where the license plate normally went. She took a deep beath, let it out slowly and put the scope at the bottom of the windshield of the red car. She mentally estimated the speed they were going so she aimed for the bottom of the windshield thinking the bullet would hit the driver. When the cars reached a mark she had picked out along the road, she pulled the trigger.

Helcom watched as the bullet went through the windshield. She could not determine if she hit the driver, but the car veered into the center portion of the large sixteen-wheeler and spun halfway around and ran off the road backwards. It flipped several times before it came to a stop, with dirt and rocks flying everywhere. The driver of the second car slammed on his brakes as soon as he saw what was happening but was too close to the lead car as it spun out of control. As it spun the lead car hit the second car and forced it between the tires of the truck's trailer. The truck's driver was trying to maintain control of his rig, but his trailer dragged the tractor off the road, across the dirt median and it rolled over blocking the oncoming lanes. The third car had his radar cruise control activated and it managed to come to a stop before it hit any of the debris in front of it. Cars began backing up in both directions of the Interstate.

Helcom wanted to stay and watch what she had caused but decided to leave the scene. She put the rifle in its case and hurriedly walked down the hill to the vehicle. As she walked, she thought about how to get back to Albuquerque because the east bound lanes will be closed along with the west bound lanes. The police would discover that a bullet caused the problem and realizing that all the cars had stopped they may begin to search, looking for the shooter. Her vehicle was a six-year-old Ford F-150 and had a flip seat where the rifle was kept. She didn't want to take the chance that she would be stopped. She had driven to the top of the hill by following a dirt road that looked as though it had not been used for quite a while. She felt that the dirt road would lead somewhere east and eventually end up on a solid surface road which would lead back to the main city. It would take longer but it would be safer.

Helcom got in the pickup and drove a quarter mile back to a dirt road that ran behind the hill from where she took the shot. She stopped the truck, got out and retrieved a broom from the truck bed and started brushing away the tire marks made when she drove to the shooting spot. In one hundred yards she stopped, walked back to the truck in a zigzag fashion, and put the broom in the truck.

If they do come up here searching for tire tracks, I don't think they will venture too far off the main road looking. She could hear the sirens as the fire trucks and other official vehicles merged on to the wrecks below. She pulled three-inch-thick chains from the back of the truck. Each chain was eight feet long and connected by a cross chain at the end. *I'll drag these chains behind my truck. They cause a lot of dust, but they will cover my tire tracks on this dirt road. I'll put them back in the truck a couple of miles down the road.*

CHAPTER FOUR

Wilt Morrison was sitting in his office trying to listen to a middle-aged man explain why he needed the services of a private detective. He noticed the man dressed in a worn sports coat, and his shoes were scuffed and worn. There was nothing expensive about the guy and Wilt knew there would be trouble with the cost per hour he charged.

"I don't know where she goes at night. She goes out and comes home a few hours later and will not tell me where she's been."

"Did you ask her where she's been?" asked Wilt.

"Yes, and she just says she's been out and don't worry about it."

"And how long has this been going on?"

"About a week," was the response.

"I'll tell you what, Mr. Uh," Wilt was searching his mind for the man's name.

"Barker, Jesse Barker," came the reply.

"I'll tell you what Mr. Barker, I charge four hundred dollars an hour for my services. You give me your address and tell me when your wife will be home, and I'll talk to her about her actions. I'll get an answer and wrap this whole thing up in an hour. Your charge will be four hundred dollars. That seem OK?"

Mr. Barker sat there for a moment. He got up from the chair he was sitting in and said, "I'll take another try at getting an answer myself. If I can't get her to talk to me, I'll let you know, and you can have a go. Thanks for your time." He turned and left.

Funny how that works. You scare them with a little money and their situation becomes much less of a problem. His wife is doing something for him and doesn't want him to know what it is. Once he threatens to spend four hundred dollars to find out, she will quickly come clean.

Wilt sat alone in his office and suddenly had an empty feeling. Occasionally, he thought of Pearl, his live in lover who was killed during his last operation. *I miss you, Pearl. I miss your advice, having a drink with you after a stressful afternoon, and holding your hand when we go for a walk. I remember how you pulled me from a deep depression after I was shot when I was a police officer in San Francisco. Had it not been for you I would have drunk myself to death. We had a wonderful time while I worked in the wine country until the people from Russell Cove started killing each other. When we moved to Albuquerque there was the serial killer after my niece, Joy, who I called my Little Butterfly. I went after the fake jewelry gang who also ran guns into Mexico. I wish you would have never gotten involved in that operation because they killed you. Damn I miss you.* Wilt took a deep breath, closed his eyes, and tried to think of something else.

He picked up the paper and there was a story of the second sniper shooting. This one took place on Interstate 40 going west. It described the pick-up being shot through the windshield and spinning out of control. It explained how the first car clipped the car following and shoving it under an oversized truck. The picture in the paper showed a semi-truck lying on its side across the westbound lanes with all lanes being closed. A quote from the officer in charge lead one to believe the shooter was on one of the nearby hills. A search of the area was progressing. Two people were killed and three were injured in the mayhem, including the driver of the lead car.

Wilt's thoughts went to the shooter who was causing a problem. He wanted to get involved with the State Police but didn't know quite how to manage the situation. He thought of calling Frank Courts who worked in the homicide division of the Albuquerque Police Department. Frank arranged to have Wilt work for the APD during the Turquoise Murder Case. *We know this guy who is shooting at people is trying to prove to somebody he's as good as a sniper. I may be able to convince the APD my experience as a Marine Corps Sniper would be of value in trying to catch this nut.*

He put in a call to Frank Courts at the homicide office of the Albuquerque Police Department.

"Courts, Homicide," was the answer.

"Frank, Wilt Morison. I have been reading about the shooter you have running around New Mexico and wondered if I could be any help?"

"Not a bad thought, Wilt. He just hit again on west Interstate 40 causing a hell of a traffic mess. The State Police are leading the investigation so it may take me a while to see if we could put you on as an advisor, like we did with the Turquoise Gang."

"This guy is a want-to-be sniper and is trying to prove to whomever told him he couldn't make it for some reason. Probably got turned down by the military."

"The State boys have checked with all the military recruiters, and nothing turned up. The Army recruiter said some mother called and inquired about her son but didn't specify what her son wanted to be. The call was traced to a burner phone so that was a dead end.

I'll tell you something that is not in the news, and is confidential, understood?"

"Understood," responded Wilt.

"Before his hits he sends us a clue in an email."

"Really? Well, I guess you can trace that computer and why isn't he caught already?"

"He's using an encrypted program. We believe it's something like TOR, which has multiple levels of encryption. I understand we'll get him, but it will take a while."

"What was the first clue?"

"It was the first two clues. It read *East is East and West is West*. What it meant was that his first targets were on Interstate forty going east, after that Interstate forty going west."

"Well, hell. There's no way you could have done anything about that even if you knew the answers before the targets were hit.

"I know. We also figured we had four days from the first hit to the second one."

"Any idea what weapon he was using?" asked Wilt.

"Ballistics said the bullet was too wrecked to be identified. It could have come from a few various rifles. We're guessing he had a tripod attached and a good high-power scope.

"So, the guy is well equipped. OK, Frank, let me know if you can get me on as an advisor, or even a hunter."

"I'll let you know in a few days, Wilt. I think there's a good chance because the last experience was a particularly good one. I'll be in touch." The phone went dead.

CHAPTER FIVE

For the next few days Wilt kept busy looking through old cases he had. He took the time to organize his desk, which was desperately needed.

Come on Frank, give me a call and let me know if I can assist the police in this sniper matter or not. A few individuals came into his office and explained their problem, but nothing that would take time. He did a stakeout for one lady looking to see if her husband was cheating on her. After five hours it turned out the husband changed jobs and didn't want to tell his wife. Wilt solved that problem for a thousand dollars and both individuals were satisfied.

The phone rang and Wilt jumped at it. He noticed it was from Frank Courts. "Frank, what's the news?"

"Your reputation precedes you Morrison. The state police welcomed your help. As before we'll pay you three quarters of your regular hourly price, and as before you will report to me."

"Isn't that a little unusual?" said Wilt. "You're with the Albuquerque Police Department and being used as a go between with the State Police?"

"It's a little unusual, but I've collaborated with them in the past and I know you. Rather than break in someone else they decided to use me. Quick and simple. By-the-way we call this department the APD, remember?"

"Yeah, yeah. OK anything from the shooter yet, like the next clue?"

"As a matter of fact, the next clue came in about an hour ago."

"Have you solved it yet?' asked Wilt.

"No. It says, *"To Lie in wait for something to approach."*

Wilt thought for a moment. "That could be anywhere in New Mexico. You could lie in wait anywhere on the turquoise trail or on the Emory Pass down toward Silver City, or ... "

"I know, I know," exclaimed Frank. "We have several people working on what the clue means. We figure we have a couple more days to find out where the sniper will be."

"Don't call him a sniper," quipped Wilt. "Call him a shooter because he's no real sniper."

"Speaking of snipers, we have someone we're going to send over to assist you in your quest to find this guy. The name is Dakota Chavez."

"Was he a sniper in the military?"

"No, Dakota completed sniper training in the Army but

decided to leave the military and go into police work. But the training is there."

"Do I have to have an assistant?" asked Wilt.

"Consensus of opinion is the assistant will help you spot and figure the distance to the target and do the other things a sniper's assistant does. Not only that but some top brass think having some-one else with you will keep you honest with the number of hours worked."

"Isn't that lovely. The big wigs don't trust me. I could tell them to shove it up their ass."

"Shake it off, Wilt. Being in the military, you know how these things work."

"Yeah, I know. Send him over and I'll get to know him before we take off on some wild goose chase. You say his name is Dakota?"

"Yes. Dakota was born in South Dakota to a Mexican Father and white Mother. Dakota has been around and is street smart. You'll like what you get. I'll send Dakota over right away. Glad you're aboard with us again Wilt. If we figure out the clue, I'll let you know."

While Wilt was waiting for Dakota Chavez to arrive, he heard a knock on the outside door. He got up and walked through the small outer office and opened the door. In front of him stood a female that was stunning. Wilt swallowed and thought: *What a gorgeous woman. The dark hair is nicely combed over her shoulder; her eyes are very dark and intelligent looking; her skin is olive and silky, and under her pants suit appears to be a genuinely nice figure.*

"Can I help you, Miss?" mumbled Wilt.

"Yes, if you are Wilt Morrison." Came the reply.

"I'll Wilt. And you are?"

"I'm Dakota Chavez, your new partner."

CHAPTER SIX

After Wilt regained his breath, he welcomed Dakota into his office. "We have some things to go over and some rules and actions that will make us a good team. Frank Courts told me you went through sniper school," asked Wilt.

"Yes, I did," Said Dakota. "The Army does not have any female snipers, but social pressure finally made them let a few females go through sniper school. Even though they would not let the graduates be snipers. Stupid thinking as far as I'm concerned."

"You went through the total training? The shooting and the running and the whole thing?"

"Yes, the whole thing. If you don't believe me I'll have the records sent over to you."

"No, no, that's not necessary, I believe you."

They spent the next two hours discussing the responsibilities of the shooter and the spotter. They had no trouble agreeing to Wilt being the shooter. As they finished their discussion Wilt asked her where she was staying.

"I have a small apartment off Tramway. It's not much but it's fine for now. One thing I wouldn't like is crossing the river every day, as that can be a drag due to traffic. That's why I rented on this side of the river."

Wilt came close to asking her if she wanted to stay in the extra room at his apartment, but thought it was a little soon to suggest that. They agreed to meet at nine o'clock the next day and Dakota left.

Wilt immediately called Frank Courts. "You son-of-a bitch, you didn't tell me that Dakota was a girl," Wilt blurted out as soon as Frank answered the phone. "You lead me to believe it was a man."

"I didn't lead you to believe it was a man, or a girl. Think about our conversation. I didn't say her, him, she, or he, I just kept using her name. If you don't want to work with her, send her back."

Wilt thought for a moment. "No, she will be fine. We have already talked about the different responsibilities and how we will us them."

"Nothing to do with her looks?"

"Go to Hell, Frank. Talk to you in the morning."

* * *

Wilt was scheduled to have dinner with Georgie at her house. He drove to the north I-25 and went north to Paseo Del Norte. He went Ease on Paseo until he reached Sandia Estates. He pulled into Georgie's house and parked in one of the three garages. The house was two stories and large. She came out to meet him.

"Hey, good looking, how was your day?"

Wilt hesitated to tell her about Dakota, so he verbally danced around it. "My day was fine. The Albuquerque Police Department or should I say the State Police, have accepted me as an advisor again, like what I did with the turquoise importing problem."

"That's great, Wilt. Does that mean you will need to travel more?"

"That depends on where the current shooter's targets are. The police gave me someone to help with the search."

"Another sniper?" asked Georgie.

"No, this is a female. The military still does not have female snipers, but the Army does let specific, qualified females go through training, I guess to appease the public."

"Really. What does she look like? Must be in decent shape."

"She's in shape but I'm not interested in anything about her except that she knows how to use a laser rangefinder, and she can climb and run."

"I certainly hope that's the case. Come on inside and let's have a drink and discuss this development."

I don't want to discuss this development, so I need to change the subject. "The shooter leaves clues that tells where his next target is."

"That's interesting. What are some of the clues?"

"The first two were pointing out the east and west interstate, which he used to shoot at a couple of cars. The last one caused a terrible crash and you probably read about it in the paper."

"Do you have another clue?"

"Yes but let me remind you that this information about clues is confidential and only the police know about it. Please keep it confidential, OK?"

"You can count on me dear," she said as she smiled at him.

They went into the great room, and both picked up their drinks. *"To Lie in wait for something to approach."* Said Wilt. "That's the current clue. The whole department is working on it."

"That's easy," said Georgie as she took a small sip of her drink. "The Indigenous translation of the Tucumcari Mountain is *to lie in wait for something to approach.* That's where Tucumcari got its name. It was originally called Rag Town, after that Six Shooter Siding. It was wild in the early nineteen hundreds."

"Are you sure? Where did you get that information?"

"I took a class in New Mexico history two months ago. For some reason, the Tucumcari Mountains stuck in my head. The whole history of New Mexico is interesting. Look what happened to Tucumcari after Rout sixty-six went through it. The whole town..."

"Sorry Georgie, dinner is off. I must get to Tucumcari as quickly as I can. It's a two-and-a-half-hour drive."

"But it's late, Wilt. What are you going to do when you get there in the middle of the night?"

"Try and figure out where the shooter is setting up for his shot. It's going to be difficult, but I need to try. Excuse me while I make a phone call." *Damn I didn't ask Dakota what her phone number is. I'll call Courts and tell him about the clue, and maybe he knows her number. It wouldn't be a good start to leave her behind on my first trip to find the shooter.*

He punched the numbers in his phone and hoped Frank was still in his office.

"Courts, Homicide."

"Frank it's Wilt. Have you solved the clue yet?"

"Just did. It's about Tucumcari."

"I know. Georgie just solved it for me. I've decided to drive to Tucumcari tonight and I'd like to take Dakota with me. Do you know what her phone number is?"

"Dakota?" said Georgie.

"I have her number in my phone." Said Frank. He gave the number to Wilt. "I'll alert the Tucumcari Police that you will be coming and please check in with them when you arrive."

"Thanks." Said Wilt and clicked off.

While Wilt was looking at his phone getting ready to put in Dakota's number. Georgie was getting rather impatient.

"Her name's Dakota?" she asked. "How old is she?"

Wilt punched in the apartment number and with his phone held in his ear, looked at Georgie and said, "I don't know. I'd guess late twenties or early thirties." He looked at her and held up his index finger motioning her to be quiet. "The phone is ringing, and I have to talk to her."

Georgie looked at Wilt, turned her back to him and started to walk into another room. She said over her shoulder, "Please be careful Wilt and don't get shot. And tell Dakota hello for me."

Wilt watched Georgie walk away and knew she was mad and hurt. *I'll deal with this later. Right now, I have more important things to do.* "Hello Dakota, this is Wilt. The shooter is going to hit his target in Tucumcari. Give me your apartment number and I'll pick you up in thirty minutes. Prepare for at least one day on the road. I'll explain more when I see you. Tucumcari? It's about three hours west from Albuquerque, toward Amarillo, Texas. I'll tell you about it on the way. I also think it would be a good idea to pack a three-day go-bag and have it handy. We may have several quick trips around New Mexico that will be overnights. Bye"

Wilt drove by his apartment and threw some clothes in a small suitcase. He picked up his gun case which housed the three hundred Winchester Magnum, the twenty-four variable power scope, the tripod for the barrel, and the silencer made special for his rifle. The case also stored two boxes of Sig Sauer 190 grain cartridges. He also made sure his laser rangefinder was tucked in the case.

It was eight o'clock when he picked up Dakota. She didn't say much for the first five minutes of the ride south on Tramway Blvd but when they turned and started east on Interstate 40, she started asking questions.

"We'll get to Tucumcari at ten thirty. What do you expect to do at ten thirty at night? How do you know the shooter will even be in or around Tucumcari?"

"Question number one. There are only a couple of places where a shooter would take a position if his target was a car. I plan to investigate both of those positions when we arrive. The second question is that the shooter leaves clues as to where he's going to be. The clue led us to Tucumcari."

"What's so special about Tucumcari?

"For one thing it's the largest town between Albuquerque and Amarillo, Texas. It became a town in 1901 when the Rock Island railroad pushed through. The next important milestone was when Route sixty-six ran right through the center of town. At one time it was very popular to stop in Tucumcari for the night. Most of the old hotels are closed now but you can see what they looked like in the forties and fifties. There have been much evidence that prehistoric dinosaurs roamed the area thousands of years ago. In fact, Tucumcari has an excellent dinosaur museum. It is also known that Apache and Comanche used to live and roam the area, and Tucumcari Mountain was a good place for cowboys to watch for Indians during their cattle drives." Wilt looked over at Dakota and she was asleep. *I guess that's for the best.* He drove on.

Wilt drove for an hour in silence. He kept thinking about the shooter and what he would do when they got into the Tucumcari area. Wilt decided that Dakota had enough sleep and shook her awake. She acted a little embarrassed but didn't say anything.

"We have another hour to drive. Why don't you tell me about South Dakota and why you went in the Army."

Dakota thought for a moment. "My dad was born in Los Angles to a Latino family. He grew up learning how to fight the gangs and ruffians who roamed the LA streets. After high school he decided to travel north and try and get away from the crime and filth of the LA area. He looked for work and finally landed a job at Mt. Rushmore cleaning up around the view area where you can see the monument. After a few years he was hired by the Monument Association and became a regular tour guide and employee."

"What about your mother?" Wilt asked.

"She loved Mr. Rushmore and visited the monument as often as she could. She was from South Dakota and got to know my father during her visits. They fell in love, got married and lived in Keystone."

"Is Keystone very large?"

"No, I think there are around three hundred and fifty people who live there. It started as a gold mining town but when the mines went dry it almost became a ghost town. The carving of the monument revived Keystone and now it's a cute lively town. It has a rustic feel to it, and you can spend a lot of time walking the streets in the summer when everything is open. It is estimated that over two million people visit the monument in the summer, and as Keystone is only two miles away from the main attraction they get a lot of business during that time.

"When I was born my mother almost died and was told she couldn't have more children. I think my father wanted a son but never told me that. He taught me how to hunt and fish, was fiercely patriotic, and always said he wished he would have joined the military when he was younger."

"Is there a high school in Keystone?" Wilt asked.

"Yes, Keystone High. When I went there the enrollment was around five hundred kids. I didn't see any future in Keystone, so after high school I spent a few years working in Sioux Falls but was not happy. Following my father's advice, I joined the Army. I was going to make a career out of the military but when I discovered they had no plans to have female snipers, I decided to leave and become a police officer."

"What did you do in the Army?'

"At first I was assigned to the Intelligent section, but that was not too interesting. I tried supply but that didn't work either. The last four years I was with the Military Police, and that was what I wanted.

"How did you get to Albuquerque?"

"I have a friend who I met in the Army who lives in Albuquerque. She loves it and persuaded me to come down and stay for a few days. The hunting and fishing is great, and the weather is super. I heard Albuquerque needed police officers, so I applied, went through the training, and here I am."

"Interesting. Welcome to New Mexico. It's a beautiful place to live and work in."

"What about you Wilt? How did you end up in Albuquerque?"

"I'm from New Mexico originally. I joined the Marines after high school and received my training in San Diego. After boot camp I came back and married my high school sweetheart and took her to California. She couldn't get used to the number of people and we ended up getting a divorce and she came back here. I tried to save my marriage and left the Corps and joined the San Diego police force. It didn't work. I married the second Mrs. Morrison, and she didn't like a cop's life either. After that divorce I moved to San Francisco and joined the SFPD."

"I understand Frisco is not so pretty anymore."

"San Francisco. No, it's not. One night I was chasing a suspected thief and he shot me in the stomach. I killed him before I passed out, but it took me months to recuperate. I became depressed and was fired from the department. I felt sorry for myself and decided to drink myself to death. A wonderful woman with whom I worked named Pearl Henderson, basically broke into my apartment, got me sober and saved my life."

"Wow, are you lucky."

"We moved to the wine area in California but had a challenging time making ends meet. We moved to Albuquerque, I got my Private Investigator's license, and here I am."

"Are you and Pearl still together?"

"No, she was killed during my last case."

"Oh, I'm so sorry. What happened?"

"That's a story for another day. We need to discuss the plan when we get to Tucumcari."

"OK. What do you have in mind?"

"When the feds built the interstate they designed it to circumvent the town. There are three exits off the I forty where one can drive into the town. One of the exits is in the middle of the town and would not be conducive for a shooter. The other two are before you get into town, one coming east and one coming west. At both places the traffic must slow down getting on and off the interstate. That's where I think the shooter will set up."

"You think we should check in with the local police before we do anything? Do they know we are coming?"

"Frank Courts told me that he would let them know about us, but checking in is a real good idea, especially in the middle of the night."

When they arrived in Tucumcari Wilt and Dakota drove to the police station. They were surprised to find all the lights were on and several police officers were coming and going out of the headquarters. Wilt and Dakota parked and walked up to the greeting clerk who was busy at his desk.

"What's going on?" asked Wilt.

"Just had a shooter at the Interstate forty and the east Route Sixty-Six interchange."

"Did he cause much damage" asked Dakota.

"Who are you two and what are you doing here this time of night?'

Wilt explained who he and Dakota were and told the clerk about their activities with the state police. Dakota showed the clerk her badge.

The clerk warmed up to them and said, "Yes, the shooter caused one car to run off the road, and another one to roll over. We searched the area, but he was gone by the time we got there. We called an all-hands-on deck but still didn't get him. We just closed Interstate forty in both directions a few minutes ago for inspections, but probably too late."

Wilt and Dakota went back to their car. Both agreed that it was too late to survey the scene and they could do their investigation in the morning. They followed the old Route 66 and found a motel called the Blue Swallow that had two available rooms and checked in.

"I think we don't have to get up too early so let's plan on finding a place for breakfast at nine tomorrow."

"Agreed. See you in the morning."

The next morning, they met at Wilt's SUV and started looking for a place to have breakfast. They decided on the restaurant _KIX on sixty-six_. After breakfast they drove to the marked off site where the Tucumcari Police had determined the placement of the shooter. Wilt and Dakota both noticed that the location had a view of the east interchange to and from Tucumcari from the Interstate 40. They introduced themselves to the office in charge of the investigation and looked for tire marks but found nothing usable as the marks looked either swept or covered up by something dragged behind the car or truck.

"My guess is we are looking for a pick-up," said one of the State Policeman who was also looking at the sight. "He has to have room for chains or some other heavy device, and a pick-up would be the best option."

"Good observation," Wilt said.

Dakota said, "What about a footprint or two around where he puts out the chains or puts them back in his pick-up. There should be prints where he stops and reorganizes."

"Let's take a walk," Wilt said to Dakota. They walked in the direction the car or pick-up had to drive to the site. After a half mile they came to the junction where the dirt trail met a paved road. It appeared the shooter stopped and the paraphernalia that was being dragged behind it was reloaded. Both Wilt and Dakota thoroughly inspected the area.

"There are several footprints around where the shooter reloaded the gear he was dragging," Wilt mentioned.

"Here is a footprint that looks fresh," called Dakota. "I don't think it's from the shooter because it's too small."

"I found a small print also," said Wilt. "You think it's some teenager that's doing the shooting?"

"That, or it's a woman."

"Good thinking Dakota. Let me check with the officer in charge and find out how many women he has investigating the crime scene. You keep looking, I'll be right back." Wilt walked to where the officer was and asked him, "How many women do you have here on the hill with you?"

"Only one, why?" was the answer.

"Was she down where the dirt road meets the asphalt?" asked Wilt.

"No, why?"

"We found some small footprints in the area I just mentioned which makes us think the shooter could be a women."

"Maybe, but until I have better proof than a footprint we are looking for a male shooter."

"OK, but could you have someone make a cast of prints around the end of the dirt road?"

"Yeah, we can do that. Draw a circle in the dirt around which prints you need casted."

"Will do. Thanks." Wilt walked back to where Dakota was waiting.

Dakota said, "We could be looking for a woman driving a pick-up. I bet she had to stop for gas somewhere in Tucumcari after driving here from Albuquerque. I talked to the officer in charge and asked him to start canvasing the fuel stations in the area. Somebody saw a woman at some filling station filling up her tank."

They walked back to the shooting area and talked to the officer in charge. He agreed to direct his men to talk to the filling stations in the area. Wilt and Dakota decided to drive back to Albuquerque and give their report to Frank Courts.

"Speaking of gas, we need to fill the tank before we start driving," mentioned Wilt.

As Wilt was filling his SUV Dakota was talking to the cashier in the snack shop. She walked out and moved over to Wilt. "Cashier said he didn't see any female getting gas in a pick-up in the last few hours. He came to work at three a.m. and works until noon."

"I was afraid we could miss her due to the time she filled up and the time of people working the station."

"What about gas receipts? Does it show the type of car or a name?" asked Dakota.

"We can check, but if it's credit it only shows the amount of gas distributed, the type of credit card, and the price per gallon. There are other numbers on the receipt, but no customer name. If she paid cash, you're back to the cashier remembering something."

They continued to stop at a few gas stations on their way back to Albuquerque but found no one who remembered seeing a woman get gas in a pick-up.

CHAPTER SEVEN

Helcom was driving back to Albuquerque, watching closely in her rear-view mirror. *I better think about making my clues more difficult. The Tucumcari police must have known I was in the area. They didn't know where I was going to set up for the shoot, but it wasn't long after I hit the target before I heard sirens. Fortunately, I knew the area and left before anyone saw me. I had just enough time to put my chains back in the truck and cover the tracks before I could see the red lights coming. Good thing I gassed up before the shoot because II heard on the radio they stopped traffic for a half hour and checked each car for sniper weapons. I don't like being in a hurry because I could miss something, even some little clue as to who I am could be fatal.*

She thought about her target. *What kind of person cheats the U. S. Government? He was standing at the counter at the shooting range waiting to pay for his shooting when she heard him talk about not paying his taxes. He said he had not paid taxes for five years and screw the government.* She thought of her uncle Rob, who joined in the Marine Corps and defended his country in Viet Nam. *This guy's a sleazebag. I need to listen more closely because he could be my next target.* She learned the sleazebag was driving to Amarillo, Texas in a couple of days on business. He planned to return as far as Tucumcari and stay the night. He told his friend he would arrive in Tucumcari just about dusk.

As usual Helcom followed her target and found what he was driving. She also waited one evening for her future target to come out of a bar after dark so she could get an idea what his headlights looked like at night. The target drove a large white pick-up that was easy to identify.

When the time came, Helcom picked her spot and waited. Luck was on her side as she located the pick-up just prior to dusk so the headlights didn't' matter. She recognized the truck and the running lights. As the target slowed down to turn off the freeway and take the road to town, she shot. She was satisfied with the hit because the pick-up never made the turn and ran off the road into a field. She quickly packed her gear, dragged her chains, threw them under the seat and headed for Albuquerque.

After two hours Helcom parked her pick-up in the garage and took her rifle into the house. She was tired but knew she had to clean her weapon before doing anything else. When she finished cleaning her rifle and put it back in her truck, she had a sandwich and went to bed.

She enjoyed leaving clues with the Albuquerque Police as not only did she challenge them with her mind, but also with her shooting. Leaving a clue and getting away with hitting her target gave her a special emotional rush. *It shows them that not only am I an excellent shot, but also a very bright person.* She now wanted to work at the range more often to try and get targets. She offered to take the place of individuals who wanted time off. It was not long before she decided on her next victim.

She was sitting in her car at the Nob Hill shopping center. She had her window rolled down on the driver's side because it was a warm day. A car rolled up and parked next to her. The driver in the next car was on his cell phone telling someone about his love child he conceived a few years ago. He explained that he does not support the child, nor even want to see the child, and no, his wife doesn't know anything about it. He mentioned that he was meeting a client the next day at Ft. Sumner, probably at the grave of Billy the Kid, to finalize a deal.

Helcom watched as the man exited the car and walked into a store. She got out and took a long look at the car next to her. She waited in her car until the man, who was now a target, got in his car and left. She had a good image of the individual and knew where he would be the next day.

After hours of research, she decided what the clue would be. She sat before her computer and made sure she was in the encrypted program and sent the clue to the APD. Satisfied she decided to drive to the area and find a good place to hide. She didn't want to take the white pick-up, so she got in her little Honda and left.

Two and a half hours later she was at her destination. She drove around the area and studied the positions where she had a good view of the target, but all the spots were too close. She also wanted concealment for her position. It took her an hour to decide where she would locate for the shooting. The escape route was just as important. There was only one road in and out of the area, which bothered her. She drove back and forth from the town to the target area keeping her eyes scanning both sides of the road. One spot she thought would work was too far away for a reliable hit, so she kept looking. Further up the road there was a small knoll which was big enough to hide her truck. She also figured there was ample foliage on top of the knoll to make her silhouette difficult to see. Helcom drove over to the knoll, got out and used her laser rangefinder to measure the distance to the target. It read two hundred and fifteen yards. *I can do this, after the shot I can get out of here before any police get to the target site. I just need to be here before the target arrives and leaves.* Satisfied, she drove back to the main road, travelled into the small town, and went through a fast foods drive through. She was back in her house in Albuquerque by the time it was dark.

The next morning there were several police standing around looking at the clue that Helcom had sent. It read: **THE JERK GOES IN A CIRCLE** – The Sniper. No one said anything but each were thinking, *What the hell could this mean?*

CHAPTER EIGHT

Wilt hesitated to call Georgie when he reached his apartment from his trip to Tucumcari. *I must get this done and it probably will not be pretty.* He punched in the numbers and waited.

"How was your trip to Tucumcari?" Georgie asked as she answered the phone.

"Somewhat productive," Wilt responded. "We think the shooter is a woman, and she dives a pick-up. That narrows it down somewhat."

"Are you coming for dinner tonight?"

"I don't think so because I'm beat from all the driving and very little sleep."

"You could also sleep here, you know."

"I know, but I wouldn't get much sleep."

"And how is Dakota? Is she going to be a good partner for you?"

Wilt thought for a moment. *Careful Wilt. Don't fall in a trap here.* "She needs experience, but I think she's smart and observant. She contributed quite a bit. So far she looks like she will work fine."

"That's nice. Well let me know when you get some rest and feel like coming over."

"I will, Georgie. Goodnight." Wilt had a tough time reading how Georgie took the news that he was not coming over tonight. *She seemed OK with it, but you never know.* He went to bed early that night and did get some good sleep.

* * *

Wilt was sitting in his office with a cup of coffee. He had the habit of getting in early after Pearl's death. One reason was that sleep became difficult so getting up early was no big deal. He also didn't like to hang around his apartment because it accentuated his loneliness. He was reading the morning paper when he heard the outer door open. He guessed it was Dakota coming in to find if there was anything new.

"You can always just call and ask me if anything is new, Dakota. You don't have to come into my office."

"I couldn't sleep either. Might as well come into the office. Any more clues?"

Wilt looked at her and again noticed how attractive she was. He even thought she was sexy in her police uniform, which she was wearing. "I don't know. No one has called me about another clue."

"Have you given your report yet?"

"Just finished and emailed it to Frank."

Just after his sentence his cell phone rang. Wilt noticed it was from Frank Courts. "Morning Frank, you get my report?"

"Yeah, but I have not read it yet. We have another clue that you and Dakota should start working on."

"The most important thing in my report is the shooter may be a woman driving a pick-up truck."

"Interesting. That narrows it to a couple thousand people," he responded.

Wilt could tell there was sarcasm in Frank's voice, and he felt a flush of anger. "You get out of the wrong side of the bed this morning?"

"Yeah, sorry. That's useful information. I'll put out that we may be looking for a women."

"I'll put my phone on speaker. Dakota is here. What's the next clue?"

"The Jerk Goes In A Circle," said Frank. We're working on it now but nothing so far.

"I'll let you go know, Frank. Keep us informed if anything comes up or the clue is solved."

Wilt wrote the clue down on a sheet of paper. Both he and Dakota were close together looking at the clue, which was lying on Wilt's desk. Wilt heard the outside door open and before he could think about who it could be, Georgie walked in.

"This must be Dakota," Georgie said. "Hi, I'm Georgie, Wilts girlfriend. In fact, I could say we are more than friends, aren't we Wilt?"

"Georgie! What are you doing over here this time of morning?"

"I had a hard time sleeping so I thought I would come by early and let you buy my breakfast."

"That's a good idea," said Dakota. "Go ahead Wilt. I'll stay here and think about the next move."

Before Wilt could say anything, Georgie said, "Do you have another clue? I solved the first one, maybe I can solve the second one. What's the clue?"

Dakota looked surprised, "You know about the clues?"

Georgie looked directly at Dakota and said, "Like I said, dear, we are more than friends."

Wilt regained his thought process and said, "OK, Georgie, let's go for breakfast. I'll tell you about the clue over scrambled eggs." He took her by the elbow and led her out of the room. Wilt could tell that Georgie was a little upset but the more he thought about it, he started getting upset. She started the conversation when they got in the car to drive to the restaurant.

"Dakota is a very pretty girl. I assume you have noticed that."

"Yes, I have noticed that. I've noticed lots of pretty girls in my life, but it doesn't mean anything. Is that why you came down here, to see what Dakota looks like?"

"I like to know if I have competition for your affection," Georgie said. "You know how I feel about you, but I'm still not sure how you feel about me."

"For one thing, I don't appreciate you checking up on me. We are in the middle of an investigation of a serial killer who goes around the state shooting people. I need to put my entire thoughts towards catching the shooter."

Wilt abruptly pulled into a parking spot near the restaurant and shut off the engine. They both sat there for a moment without looking at each other.

"I'm sorry if I've upset you. I didn't see you two nights ago, and I didn't see you last night. I miss you and wanted to see how you were doing, and at least have breakfast with you. If you want to take me back to my car, that's fine," said Georgie.

Wilt felt some of his anger fade as his heart slowed down and his breathing became deeper. "Georgie, you know I have strong feelings for you. You have helped me immensely when Pearl passed, which

I really appreciate. You are attractive, smart, fun, and sexy. I still feel an emptiness since Pearl died and until I can control that feeling I can't commit to another relationship."

"I understand because I had the same feeling when Jack was killed. But I'm sure that both Jack and Pearl would want both of us to continue our lives and be happy."

They exited the car and walked into the restaurant. Once they ordered their breakfast, Wilt continued. "The next clue is *The Jerk Goes In A Circle.* To my knowledge no one has solved it yet."

Georgie was silent for a moment. "That's another easy one. The capital building for New Mexico in Santa Fe is circular. In fact, it is the only round capital building in the United States. Inside, as you know, are hundreds of artworks done by local artists. Tourists and local New Mexicans spend hours going through this unique building just to view the pictures and other types of art."

"What's that have to do with the clue?" asked Wilt.

"Some people think politicians are jerks. The building is round. The jerk goes in a circle means the shooter is going to kill one of the politicians in Santa Fe, or maybe the Governor."

Wilt thought about what Georgie said. "I guess it's possible, and what you say makes sense." He hit the speed dial on his phone and waited for Frank Courts to answer.

"You've reached Frank Courts of Homicide, please leave a message." Wilt had forgotten how early it was.

Wilt waited for the signal. "Frank, Wilt Morrison here. Georgie has come up with a pretty good idea about the clue. Give me a call when you get in. The governor could be in danger."

"Let's get back to our previous discussion," urged Georgie. "I want you to promise me that if you start having feeling for anyone else that you will tell me."

"That's a difficult promise to make. We could go round and round discussing the definition of the word FEELINGS."

"You know exactly what I mean, Wilt. I just don't want to get so deep in this relationship that you break my heart. I think I can control my affection to a certain level and keep my guard up until I'm sure you are ready to commit."

"Does this mean we can date other people?"

"No! If you start dating other people we are done."

"Let's get some desert."

The desert station was in the corner of the room. It was a soft service ice cream machine that distributed vanilla, chocolate, or a combination of the two into small cones. As Wilt moved to fill his cones, Georgie moved close, and he felt her breast against his arm. He could not help himself and became aroused.

"No fair Georgie. You know what that does to me."

"Just testing Wilt. Glad it still works."

* * *

Back at the office parking lot Wilt said goodbye to Georgie and walked up to his office. Dakota was sitting on the visitor's side of his desk looking at her laptop. She lifted her head and looked at him and said, "Good breakfast?"

"We got a few things settled; I think. May even have an answer to the clue."

"Really. I've been working on that also and have a couple of ideas about it."

Wilt told Dakota about what Georgie has said about the capital building. Dakota thought it was very interesting and told Wilt next time she was in Santa Fe she would be sure to visit the building.

"Another interesting thing about the capital is before the last session it was legal to carry a concealed weapon into the building if you had a concealed carry permit. The thinking was if anyone came in with the intent of doing harm and pulled a gun he or she would be outgunned. It was reputed to be the safest place in New Mexico," said Wilt.

"Why'd they change it?"

"Liberals thought it was too risky with all the semiautomatic rifles available. They may have been right, and the restriction of no guns allowed was approved. Now you need to go through a metal detector to get in the building."

Dakota was silent for a moment, then said, "I took a different tact in looking at the clue. I got on Google and started asking questions about circles in Spanish. I didn't get much out of that and could not relate anything to the clue. I tried JERK and circle around jerk, and I still came up with nothing that I could use. It must be some word in Spanish that has something to do with both circles and jerk."

"I think you are on the right track," said Wilt. "Try changing the words in the clue. For example, use stupid rather than jerk, or square rather than circle, and keep changing words until you come up with something that will fit."

The two of them sat at Wilt's desk for the next two hours playing a word game. They changed the words but tried to still have a similar meaning. They took the word circle and tried ring, loop, sphere, disc, ball and finished on round.

Dakota gave out a little squeal, "I have a hit. Round in Spanish is Redondo. I know there are a few areas called Redondo in New Mexico"

"Yes, there is the Jemez Redondo, which is a mountain in the Jemez Forest. Also, there is the Bosque Redondo near Fort Sumner where the state built a monument to the Navajo Long Walk."

Wilt's phone rang. Wilt saw that it was Frank Courts. "Morning Frank. Thanks for the call back."

"What the hell are you talking about, killing the governor?"

"It was Georgie. She thought about the clue and said many people think politicians are jerks and the state capital is round, so there are jerks running around in the circle in Santa Fe. Makes sense to me. I think it's worth acting on."

"Well, it may be the best we have right now. Are you going to the round house and stand guard and wait for the shooter?"

"No," Wilt said. "The shooter is smarter than that. There is no escape route around there and the field of fire is lousy. I think that's a long shot, no pun intended."

"You got anything better?"

"Dakota and I are working on the possibility of the Bosque Redondo area. According to Google there is a saying about a Redondo Jerk. The terrain around Fort Sumner is superior for a longer shot, and the accessibility in and out of the place is better. Maybe the shooter is looking to kill a Forest Ranger, or a tourist, or someone visiting Billy the Kid's grave."

"Shall I alert the Fort Sumner Police?"

"You can tell them Dakota and I will be in the area, but it is a long way from being a sure thing." Wilt clicked off and turned to Dakota, "We might as well get going on over to Fort Sumner because we don't know when the shooter is going to hit if he or she hits that area. Once again, take enough clothes for a couple of nights. We'll either stay in Santa Rosa or Fort Sumner."

"What kind of place is Bosque Redondo?" asked Dakota.

"I'll tell you all about it on the way there."

* * *

Once again Wilt took Interstate 40 east toward the town of Santa Rosa. As he was driving he told Dakota the story of Bosque Redondo.

"You must go back to the Civil War to talk about the history of Bosque Redondo. A man by the name of General Carleton was charged with stopping the raids of Mescalero Apache and Navajo Indians. There was real frustration within the U.S. Government about these two tribes from the Spanish and Mexicans who were living in New Mexico. General Carleton first chose a site to house and guard five thousand Indians in a place called Bosque Redondo. This area had the Pecos River running through it and a lot of greenery. The General thought it would be a good place for the Indians to live and thrive. He built a fort on the property, called it Ft. Sumner, and ordered Col Kit Carson to carry out a plan to force the Indians to come to Bosque Redondo. Carson wanted to resign from the Army because he didn't want to have to treat the two tribes as the enemy and force them to live in the Redondo. The General refused his resignation, so Carson carried out his plan.

"First were the Apache. Carson's orders were to kill all the adult males and march the women and children to the Bosque, which was several miles from where the Apache were camped. The Mescalero chief knew that Carson had the men to carry out his order and

51

surrendered. About five hundred of the Apache were marched to the Bosque and lived there under guard from the solders in the fort.

"The Navajo's were different. The only way Carson could gather the Navajo was to burn their food sources every time he and his troops found a growing area. Eventually seven thousand Navajo men, women, and children marched an average of three hundred and fifty miles from their homes in northern New Mexico to the Bosque Redondo. Many died on the march, and many were shot by the troops if they could not keep up. The Navajo call it *The Long Walk* and blame Carson for the torture and demise of many men, women, and children."

"I know the Navajo have their own nation now, how did they get out of the Redondo?" asked Dakota.

"They made a treaty after trying to live in the Bosque for five years. In 1868 the remaining Navajo walked back to their agreed upon area, which was smaller than the original reservation and they live there today. The Navajo Nation is mostly in Arizona, but some of the land is in New Mexico. It's about the size of West Virginia."

"Is there anything left of the Bosque Redondo?" She asked.

"The story continues. After the Indians left, the solders left the area, and a flood took out most of the structure of the fort. The only thing left was the officer's quarters. In the 1860s Lucien Maxwell, who sold his land in Colfax County, bought the officer's quarters and much of the land around the fort. He built a large home using some of the officer's quarters and called it the Maxwell Ranch. He started the town now known as Fort Sumner. The interesting thing about the Maxwell Ranch is a man by the name of Billy the Kid was smitten by one of the Maxwell daughters and would come up and visit the ranch. Pat Garret found out about Billy's visits and caught him in one of the rooms and shot him."

"Isn't there some question about who was shot?"

"Yes, but most think it was Billy the Kid. I'll tell you my opinion. Last year I met the great grandson of Lucien Maxwell, who authored a book about Lucien. When he was a child he remembers talking to his great aunt about the shooting before she died. The aunt lived at the Maxwell Ranch and knew Billy due to his visits. His aunt remembers seeing Billy after he was shot, and she said there was no question it was Billy."

"Is Billy buried near the Maxwell Ranch?" asked Dakota.

"He was, but during the flood 1904 that took out the Maxwell Ranch house, also took Billy's body down the river. No one knows what happened to it or where it is. The headstone is there but without Billy's body."

"What's left at the Bosque Redondo?" asked Dakota.

"In two thousand and five the New Mexico Historical Sites and some museums got together and decided to build a memorial to the native American who were interned at this reservation. The Navajos also participated financially. A beautiful building was constructed with murals and pictures about the Long Walk and the time the Indians were there. There is also a self-tour you can take around the grounds. It's interesting to visit and if we have the time on this trip we'll walk through the memorial and look at Billy the Kid's grave."

"Is the town of Fort Sumner very large?"

"Population is around fifteen hundred people. Main attraction is the Billy the Kid Museum. You'll see it as we go through the town on our way to the Bosque Redondo."

"What does the word Bosque stand for? Is it French? "asked Dakota.

"Bosque is Spanish for *Forest*. It usually describes the trees on either side of a river."

"Well, let's hope we got the clue correct, and can get this shooter person."

CHAPTER NINE

Helcom cleaned her rifle and made sure it was in good firing order by snapping the trigger four times. She put the weapon under the seat of her truck, started the vehicle, checked the fuel gauge, and began her trip to Fort Sumner. *I wonder if anyone has figured out the clue yet? Even if they did they would not know if I'm going to hit a car, or a person. They don't even know if I'm going to kill someone at the grave of Billy the Kid, or a guide at Bosque Redondo.*

She turned on to Interstate 40 and headed east toward Santa Rosa. It was dark by the time she turned off Interstate 40 onto Highway 84 toward Fort Sumner. The next forty-five miles were easy as there was little traffic in either direction. Helcom drove through the sleepy town of Fort Sumner and turned right on Billy the Kid Drive. She started looking for the knoll she discovered two days ago which would hide her pick-up. She found the turn-off. Even though it was dark, she dropped her chains from the back of her truck and dragged them from where the dirt road began to where she parked the pick-up. The brush on the top of the knoll would hide her rifle and make it hard to see her from the distance of Billy the Kid's grave. She set up her equipment and went back to the pick-up to get some sleep before the sun came up. She had time to think about what her actions would be after the shot was fired. *First the direction of the shot is south, and the sun comes up in the east, so no possibility of any reflection on the rifle scope. The terrain is flat around here so people at the grave who hear the shot will be a little confused as to which direction it came from. Also, the target will be hit and drop to the ground before the sound of the shot reaches the graveyard and if I'm lucky most of the people will have their attention on the fallen target, not which direction the sound came from. One problem will be the dust that will be in the air behind me if I drag the chains to cover my tracks. A dust cloud could show where I'm coming from. If I don't cover my tracks, and they find the right road, a cast of the tracks could be taken. I must take that chance and not use the chains. Maybe they will take the wrong road. I also must put the chains under the driver's seat with the rifle in case they want to search the cars in the area. I need to get through Fort Sumner and on to Santa Rosa before the law closes the roads.* She wanted to keep thinking about the escape but fell asleep.

The bright sun shining on her face woke her up. She had a few sips of coffee and took her binoculars and surveyed her surroundings. Satisfied there was no one in sight, she walked to the bottom of the knoll and crawled up to the top where she left her rifle. She set her scope to twenty-four power and focused in on the grave of Billy the Kid. It was early and no one was around. She moved back down the knoll, had some more coffee and waited.

* * *

Wilt and Dakota entered Fort Sumner an hour before it got dark. They stopped at Super 8 Wyndham and were in luck with two separate rooms.

"I think we need to start getting reservations before we leave Albuquerque," Dakota said. "We won't be this lucky all the time."

Wilt thought, *That would be nice. Why am I thinking that?* "How about breakfast at eight o'clock? I checked and the graveyard doesn't open until nine o'clock, which will give us plenty of time to get there."

"What if the target is at the Bosque Redondo?"

"I thought about that, and I think the best thing to do is to split up. You take the Bosque and I'll take the graveyard."

"That's a good idea, except for the fact that if someone is shot at the bosque I'll need to contact you and by the time we get together the shooter will be gone," explained Dakota.

"What do you suggest?"

"Let's pick one or the other. At least that way we can react together once the target is hit. If we're at the graveyard it will only take a few minutes to get to the bosque. We can tell the guides to contact us if anything unusual happens."

Wilt thought for a moment, "Shall we tell them about the potential shooter?"

"That would be great and have them all run for their cars. No, we need to keep that close to the chest."

"OK, the graveyard it is, and both together."

Before Wilt went to bed he called the Fort Sumner Police Station and checked in. The officer that answered the phone told him Frank Courts had called and they are aware of their mission. The officer also said they would have a car on standby until noon if anything happened at the gravesite or the Bosque. He gave Wilt his private number and told him to get in contact if he's needed. That ended the phone conservation.

At eight o'clock the next morning Dakota came down to the breakfast area and found Wilt already sitting at a small table. Wilt looked up and saw Dakota dressed in a white blouse and slacks. Her police badge was hooked to her belt on the right hip. She looked very nice.

"You look nice this morning," Wilt said. "I think that outfit is better than your uniform. We don't want to scare off the shooter."

Dakota went to the coffee urn and poured herself a cup. She put a yogurt on her plate and came back to the table.

"Did you notify the local police that we are here?" she asked.

"That's all taken care of. They will have a car standing by until noon. If anything happens it should be before noon."

After a mediocre breakfast they drove out past the graveyard and went on to the Bosque Redondo.

"Wow, that's a beautiful building," said Dakota when she saw the memorial.

"The history I gave you in our trip down here is just the tip of the iceberg," explained Wilt. "There is much more to the story which you can find on the Internet. I wanted you to see the outside of this building before we parked ourselves at the graveyard. In the future you can come back and spend time going through the building and take a self-guided tour of the grounds."

"I'll have to do that. What an interesting place."

They drove back to the graveyard and parked. There were three other people there walking around the graves. Dakota walked up to the headstone of Billy the Kid and said, "I can guess why the grave marker is behind a fence so you can't get close."

"The headstone has been stolen at least three times. I think the last time it ended up in California. People do crazy things."

* * *

Helcom was watching the five people at the gravesite through her rifle scope. She kept looking for her target to arrive. She didn't see the car the target was driving and began to wonder if her target changed his mind about being here. She took particular interest in the couple who drove up last. The tall man kept looking around past the fenced-in yard into the horizon. He seemed to be looking for some distant object. *I really don't like the looks of that guy. He must be looking for a reflection off my scope. I better rethink this shot. It could be difficult to get out of here if they already know my target. Maybe I could drop him as the target. He has some woman with him who is also looking at everything except the grave.* Helcom crawled off the top of the knoll and took her equipment back to the truck. She sat in the pick-up for fifteen minutes trying to determine her next move. She wanted to hit a target this morning but was worried about her escape route. She was thinking about driving back through Fort Sumner on highway 84 toward Santa Rosa. *Screw it. I came here to shoot someone and that's what I'm going to do. The guy who is continually looking around is now the target. Sorry buster, your curiosity just got yourself killed.*

Helcom unpacked her rifle and equipment and crawled back to the top of the hill. Once set up she put her cross hairs from her scope on the head of the taller man looking around the graveyard. While he was looking in her direction and the crosshairs were on the center of his forehead, she pulled the trigger.

* * *

Wilt and Dakota had been at the graveyard for over two hours. Both thought they may have made the wrong choice of location.

Nothing was heard from Bosque Redondo either, which could indicate they misread the clue. While they were looking at each other wondering what to do next, Wilt's cell phone rang. He looked down and saw it was Georgie calling. For a second he thought he would not take it but decided to talk to her.

Wilt looked at Dakota and said, "I have to take this." He turned away to walk to a more private area when he felt a breeze of air fly by his head. Simultaneously a loud noise came from the headstone behind him, and he heard the shot. He turned and looked at Billy the Kid's headstone and immediately deduced that it was hit by a bullet. *Sniper!*

He yelled, "Sniper, everybody get down or behind something." He grabbed Dakota by the waist and pulled her behind the SUV. They both looked at each other not saying anything but knew they were temporarily safe. Wilt could hear Georgie yelling at him through the phone. He put the phone to his mouth and said, "I'm OK Georgie. I'll call you back," and clicked off. They both slowly raised their heads and looked over the hood of the SUV, through the front and back windows, trying to see anything that could tell them the location of the shooter. Wilt was confident the shooter could not see them through the tented car windows. He thought he saw some dust coming from a few hundred yards away but wasn't sure.

"Do you think she'll shoot again if she can get a bead on us?" asked Dakota.

"It depends on the escape route. If she is comfortable with waiting a few minutes yes, she'll try again. If we sit here for three minutes she will be gone." He looked at his phone and hit the number for the police in Fort Sumner. He identified himself and told the dispatcher that a few minutes ago the shooter tried to hit him but missed. She is probably on the road back to Fort Sumner driving a pick-up. Please try to intercept her before she gets through town.

"We'll be on our way from here."

"What the hell was that? Did you say sniper? Did you know someone was going to try to shoot us?" asked a man from in front of the adjacent car.

"The sniper didn't try to shoot anyone but me." Wilt said.

People started to get out from behind their cars and walk toward Wilt and Dakota. There were two families of four people each. Dakota stepped in front of Wilt, pulled her badge off her belt, and showed it to the small group.

"I'm an Albuquerque Police Officer and we suspected a person would be in this area who is going around the state shooting at people. We also suspected he or she may try to shoot an officer of the law, not just anyone. We believe none of you were in any danger but when the shooter missed the primary target we thought he or she might shoot again just to hit anyone, that's why we told you to take cover."

Wilt stood by Dakota and said, "The shooter is trying to get out of the area now. We need to try and catch this monster before someone else gets shot. You will have a story to tell your friends tonight. Enjoy the rest of your day." He moved to his SUV, followed by Dakota, and they both entered the vehicle and started to leave. The two families were talking among themselves, seemingly forgetting about the man who was the target.

* * *

Helcom saw the tall man's head move just as she pulled the trigger. *Shit, he moved.* She saw the bullet hit the headstone which caused the people around the grave to move back toward their cars. She quickly deduced that there wasn't any time for a second shot due to the flat terrain around the area. *I need to get out of here as quickly as I can. They may close the roads back to Fort Sumner and if they do that, I'm stuck.* She moved as quickly as she could, took apart the rifle and put it under the seat. She started to pull the chains out to use, thought better of it and put them back. *They'll cast my tire marks, and my shoe prints. I'll purchase some used tires when I get back to Albuquerque, and I'll change my shoes.* Finished, she got in the pick-up and started for the main road. As she neared the road she heard a siren and stopped. She put the pick-up in reverse and backed up a little further off the road. She watched the police car go screaming by toward Bosque Redondo, neither police officer was looking any direction except forward. *Well, it's my lucky day. I'll wait for a minute and the cop car will be out of sight and I'll head toward Fort Sumner and go on to Albuquerque. They will not close the roads until they get to the graveyard or Bosque Redondo and realize I was nowhere near either location. They will decide I'm getting away and might try and close the roads. But no one was injured. They may not want to disturb the shoppers visiting Fort Sumner by making such a drastic move. They might just look for me by putting cars on the road. In any case I need to keep driving, and after I get through Fort Sumner I'll stay within the speed limit so hopefully I will not be stopped.*

Helcom kept driving and glancing at her rear-view mirror. She made the turn from highway 84 to north on Interstate 40. She was glad she had the foresight to get gas in Santa Rosa when she came down yesterday. *No need to stop as I can make it all the way home with what I have in the tank. First thing tomorrow I'll get some tires and shoes.*

As she drove her mind went to her target back at the graveyard. *I need to find out who that guy was. The way he and his girlfriend were looking around I bet they thought I was in the area. I have not read where the police have mentioned anything about the clues I leave before the shooting. That being the case, those two must be with the local police. I need to find out who he is and where he lives. He may be my next target.*

CHAPTER TEN

Wilt and Dakota were driving at a high rate of speed toward Fort Sumner when they passed a police car going the other way toward Bosque Redondo. Wilt got on his phone and told the Bosque Redondo guide that when the police arrived there to redirect them to the graveyard. He turned the car around and started back toward the Graveyard. He called Georgie back and told her what was going on around him.

"Your call saved my life. If I hadn't moved to talk to you I'm sure the bullet would have found its mark."

"My God, Wilt. What were you doing down there, just waiting to be shot?"

"No, we thought maybe the shooter would try to hit a moving car, like she did before. We didn't expect her to shoot at a stationary person."

"Why did she shoot at you? Weren't there other people around you?"

"That's a good question, Georgie. Let me think this over and we can talk about it at dinner tonight, if I'm still invited."

"Of course, you're invited. Try to make it back to Albuquerque in one piece. I'll expect you as soon as you can get here."

"OK, Georgie. I need to go now. We've caught up with the police car and we need to talk to them." He clicked off. The police were standing outside their car talking to one of the families that were still at the graveyard.

Wilt and Dakota walked over to the group, introduced themselves, and Wilt asked the police officers, "Did you see a pick-up driven by a woman on your way here?"

"Over half of the pick-ups in this county are driven by women," responded the officer. "We were told to high tail it to Billy the Kid's gravesite, and that's what we did."

"The shooter was somewhere along the road back to Fort Sumner," explained Wilt. "We need to try and find where she went off the main road to set up the shoot. Plus, we need to stop her before she gets to Santa Rosa because I'm sure she is going to try to go all the way back to Albuquerque today. Can you set up a roadblock on highway eighty-four just before you get to Interstate forty?"

The same officer looked at Wilt and at Dakota. "Setting up a roadblock like you asked isn't an easy task. It'd take a couple of hours to get everyone together and get the thing properly active. By that time, she'd be long gone. Nope, we're not going to do that. We'll help you look for her exit and entry spots along the road back, though. What'd you do if you find her tracks?"

"I'd ask you or someone you designate to make a casting of the tracks. If we find the pick-up we'd check the tires to the casting to see if we have a match."

"OK," the officer said. "Let's go hunting."

Wilt started for his SUV, stopped, and turned around. "First let me see if anything is left of the bullet that hit Kid's headstone. We still have not identified the caliper of bullet she's using." He quickly walked over to the cage that surrounded the headstone. "Any way to get past this cage so I can take a close look at the headstone?"

The officer shrugged his shoulders and said, "I guess we could ask the person inside the information office, but I'm sure the bullet is blown to little pieces."

Wilt gave up. "You 're probably right. OK, let's go find some pick-up tracks."

They started back toward Fort Sumner looking for dirt roads that led eastward off the main road. They found three, one of which had fresh tire marks pressed into the loose dirt.

"This has to be the road she used." Wilt said. "It's less than a thousand yards from the graveyard."

Dakota was following the road with her eyes. "Looks like a berm or knoll over there." As she pointed down the road.

After more discussion, the officer in charge agreed to take some castings of the tire marks and of the boot prints that were in the dust.

"Wonder why she didn't use the chains to cover her tracks and boot prints," Wilt asked, almost to himself.

"She didn't think she had the time," Dakota said. "I think we can assume she plans to purchase some new or used tires, which will make the castings useless."

"Good point," said the officer in charge. "No need to cast these so let's forget about that."

Wilt conceded, "That's probably what she'll do, so yeah, drop the idea of the tire castings. We still need the footprints, though, because even if she changes shoes the size will be the same. It's just one more thing that may lead us to the right person."

"Will do," was the response.

Wilt and Dakota thanked the officers and decided to head for home. They stopped in Fort Sumner to have some lunch since it was midday. Not knowing which eating place to choose, they stopped at Rodeo Grill.

After they sat down, Wilt looked at Dakota, got her attention and said, "You did a smart thing back at the graveyard. Stepping in front of one of the families and showing them your badge was good thinking. That surprised and relieved them knowing they had a police officer in their midst. In fact, Dakota I had my doubts at first, but now I'm glad you came aboard as my partner."

On the way home after an excellent lunch, Dakota was quiet for most of the ride, but decided to talk about the day.

"You do understand how complicated it is to set up a roadblock?" she asked.

Wilt knew, but he said, "No, tell me how complicated it is."

"Well, first the responsible individual must understand exactly what the target is and why. Plus, he or she needs to get all the participants together and explain to them the objective of the block, the time of the block and the location. There needs to be a safety coordinator that sets up the signs or flares to slow and stop traffic. The state police and any other involved organization will be notified, as well as the road commission. A roadblock is not an activity that can be thrown together in a few minutes.

"I know," said Wilt. "Maybe I spoke too soon but I thought it was a good idea at the time.

"How many used tire shops are there in Albuquerque?" she changed the subject.

Wilt thought for a moment, "I don't know. I'd guess four or five, plus a few in Rio Rancho, right across the river."

"I think we should alert every one of them to be on the lookout for a woman with a pick-up that wants to purchase some used tires."

"Good idea. I'll talk to Frank Courts about it, and he can arrange the search."

Dakota thought for a moment, "I guess we can't contact every shoe store in town and ask them to let us know if a woman comes in to buy shoes."

"No, I don't think so. I wonder if the shooter is smart enough to buy tires in another town except Albuquerque or Rio Rancho?"

"I guess she could go to Santa Fe, or south to Santa Rosa or Tucumcari. I bet she stays local."

"I hope we find out."

* * *

After Wilt dropped off Dakota and watched her walk to her apartment, he went back to his place. He changed clothes and called Frank Courts. He explained Dakota's idea about alerting the tire shops about a woman purchasing used tires. Frank thought it was a good idea and said he'd get right on it. Wilt was ready to drive over to Georgie's for dinner. He didn't know quite what to expect because he hadn't seen her for two days and he was with Dakota the whole time. He thought of Dakota. *She is turning out to be a good partner. She's smart, handles herself well, and takes advantage of her training. She is competent and humble at the same time. I like her. I also owe Georgie a lot. She really helped me after Pearl died. Did she do that for me or for herself? I hope this doesn't get more complicated because I need to focus on the shooter. Here's Georgie's house. I need to be careful what I say and how I handle this. I don't think I want to have my relationship with Georgie to get too deep, but I'm not sure.*

Georgie welcomed Wilt with a hug and a long kiss. They walked into the great room. "Great to see you, and glad that you are in one piece. That noise over the phone scared the hell out of me. Exactly what happened?"

"The shooter took a shot at me at the same time you called. I turned my head just enough that the bullet missed and hit the headstone of Billy the Kid."

"It was fate, Wilt. I know I was directed to make that call when I did. You and I were meant to be together. I think you should move in with me, and the next step would be getting married."

"It may have been fate, but maybe it was timing, I don't know. I do know that I'm still grieving over Pearl and until I get over her passing I can't commit to completely give myself to another."

Georgie looked up at Wilt with watery eyes. "I understand, but it's been six months. I've gotten over Jack in that span of time. When do you think you'll do the same? I love you Wilt, and I want you here. When will you have enough room in your heart for me?"

Damn, I hate these conversations. I don't want to hurt her but I'm just not sure it would be good overall. What's wrong with me? She's almost everything I want, but the fit just isn't right yet. "Just give me a little more time, Georgie. I'm sure we'll work this out soon."

"I'm not getting any younger either, please remember that. OK, let's have a drink and I'll get dinner. Can you stay the night?"

"I'd really like to, but I've been driving all day and I have an early appointment tomorrow with Frank Courts. I think it would be best if I stayed tomorrow night."

Georgie frowned. "I can wait another day. Tell me more about Fort Sumner and Bosque Redondo."

The conversation centered on the search for the shooter, tire tracks, and shoe prints. They had dinner and afterward Wilt left for his apartment.

CHAPTER ELEVEN

Helcom was relieved when she drove into her apartment parking lot and stopped in her familiar spot. She was nervous while driving all the way home from Fort Sumner. She didn't know if the police would set up a roadblock. Once she passed Santa Rosa she was sure she was in the clear. Relaxed, she started to think about the day's activities. *What could go wrong with my quick exit? One thing for sure is they will find where my truck was parked, or where it went on and off the main road. They may even cast my tires, and maybe even my shoe size. I had best get a different set of tires tomorrow. If they look closely at my shoe size they may discover I'm a female. Should I trade in my pick-up for a used SUV? That would keep them off my trail for longer than they anticipated. I could carry the chains in the back, and they would be enclosed. I'd have to go to Santa Fe, or Las Cruces to make the transaction because I'm sure the police will be on the lookout for any trade that involved a pick-up. That's what I'll do, drive to Las Cruces to get an SUV. Santa Fe is too close to Albuquerque. After that I'll think about my next shot.*

As she drove toward Albuquerque she began to plan where her next shot would be. She wanted it to be a well-known place, and one that would draw out the tall guy who she tried to shoot at the graveyard.

The next day Helcom left Albuquerque early headed for Las Cruces. The trip would take a little over three hours going south on Interstate 25. She would get gas in Truth or Consequences, which was halfway to Las Cruces. She thought about the way the town got its name. *Truth or Consequences, otherwise known as T or C, was originally named Hot Springs. In 1950 Ralph Edwards put out a notice that any town that changed its name to Truth or Consequences would host his successful radio program in that town once a year. Each year thereafter for fifty years Edwards traveled to T or C and celebrated the Truth or Consequences Fiesta.* As Helcom continued her trip south from T or C she thought, *I'm sure the name change really pissed of a lot of interstate sign makers. Takes a big sign to get Truth or Consequences printed on it.*

She stopped and got gas, making sure no one got a good view of her face. She paid cash and even when she stepped in front of the cashier she kept her head down, with her hat pulled down in front of her face. The cashier didn't seem to think much about it. She continued her trip, thinking she would get a car from a seller like Car Max or Carvana.

She was disappointed when she saw what was available in the town. She thought about buying a newspaper but remembered she had a pickup to trade in and she didn't think anyone in the paper would want to trade. So, she drove to El Paso, Texas, which was only forty-four miles away and a much bigger town. There she found two substantial used car dealers and traded her pickup for an SUV, plus some of her cash. She started home and discovered she needed gas.

Cheap sons-of-bitches didn't even fill my tank with gas. So, once again she had to disguise herself a little when she filled up the car.

It was late when she drove into her two-car garage. She was tired and hungry but wanted to load the SUV with chains and other sniper paraphernalia before she went into the house and ate something and went to bed. Tomorrow she would figure out where her next shot would be and how she would structure the clue.

* * *

"We've got our next clue," Frank Courts said as Wilt picked up the phone from his pocket, put it on speaker and answered it.

"I'm in my office with Dakota. Really, what is it?"

"The Youngest daughter of Estrada was disappointed," replied Frank. "We have people looking into it right now but so far we haven't figured it out."

"I assume if you find out who Estrada is the answer will come pretty quickly."

"You have any idea how many people with the name Estrada there are in New Mexico?"

"No, but I'll bet you're going to tell me, "said Wilt.

"Based on name statistics, there're twenty-eight people named Estrada for each one hundred thousand population. New Mexico has roughly two million people which means there're five hundred and sixty people named Estrada in New Mexico."

"You're lucky we're not in California because there must be thousands. Do you want me to start checking some of the names with you?"

"Checking for what? If you find someone named Estrada what do you do? How do we find out which Estrada is in the sights of the shooter? What kind of things puts a certain person in line to be shot?"

Wilt thought for a moment. "I've always assumed that the targets were random, but the places where they were shot were chosen. Maybe it's not that way. Maybe the targets were picked beforehand, and the places were random."

Dakota Chavez said, "I think you start with finding out which Estrada has at least three daughters because the young**est** was the one disappointed. If there were only two daughters the clue would have said youn**ger** daughter, assuming the shooter knows his or her grammar."

"That's some good thinking Dakota. I'll pass that along to the think tank," said Courts.

"We'll work on it from this end and let you know if we come up with something,"

"OK Wilt. I'm guessing we have maybe two days to get the answer if we have any chance of getting the perp." Frank said as he clicked off the phone.

Wilt and Dakota sat and looked at each other for a moment. She started to say something but closed her mouth as she thought it was better not to say anything first.

"You were going to say something, what was it?" asked Wilt.

Dakota looked at him, "If we think out of the box we have to assume this Estrada is either alive, or he could be dead. So, the idea is to look for any Estrada, alive or dead, that has three or more daughters. In fact, it is possible that this Estrada may not even live in New Mexico. What if he or she lived outside of the state and his disappointed daughter lives in New Mexico."

"You just expanded the search to the whole U.S.A."

"Or even Mexico or South America and maybe Spain."

I really like the way this girl thinks. "Let's put ourselves in the mind of the shooter. The clue can't be so broad that it can't be solved in some kind of short time frame."

"OK, what famous person in New Mexico was named Estrada and had at least three daughters? And why was she disappointed?"

Wilt thought for a moment. "You're the female, what one thing could disappoint a woman enough that other people would know about it?"

Dakota looked up toward the ceiling, "Probably something to do with a guy. Jewelry could be a reason, but it wouldn't be so noticed. Either this daughter was jilted or left at the alter or something happened that was terrible enough that everyone knew or knows about it."

"OK, let's recap. We're looking for a third or fourth daughter that was or is well known enough that most people would know if something happen to her that she would be disappointed. That's simple enough," said Wilt with some sarcasm in his voice.

"If most people would know about it, why don't we know about it?"

Wilt thought for a moment, "Maybe we know about it but don't know we know about it."

"What?" asked Dakota.

"I'm just thinking out loud. I'm trying to think of an example. Let's say there was a well-known event in history that we all knew about. For example, on September eleventh the world trade centers were taken down. We all knew that. If someone put in a clue about five Muslims that did something terrible we might think it was recent, but the answer would be something that happened years ago. So, some daughter whose father was Estrada may have been disappointed in something years ago."

"Let me see what I can do with Google," said Dakota as she sat down on the floor and opened her laptop.

"What are you doing on the floor?" asked Wilt.

"I can spread out down here and put the laptop in my lap. For me it's comfortable."

Wilt looked at her as she moved to cross her legs and position the laptop between them. He felt a flash of warmth spread through his loins. *She really is a good-looking woman. Smart too. No, I can't think this way, she's a temporary partner and I'm involved with another woman. Yet there is something about Dakota Chavez that gives me a warm feeling, plus it's hard to take my eyes off her.*

Five minutes later Dakota said, "The wife of Francisco Vazquez de Coronado was Beatriz de Estrada, think there is any connection there?"

"Does it say anywhere that she was disappointed in her marriage?"

"It says that Coronado came back unsuccessful in his quest for the seven golden cities. In fact, he was tried for cruelty to the native Indians he encountered but was acquitted. He ended up poor and not respected. I would think his wife would be disappointed in him toward the latter part of their marriage. There is also a wealth of information about Erik Estrada, the guy who played a CHP in the television series CHIPS."

"Did he have any daughters?" asked Wilt.

"He had one daughter from a third marriage, born in the year two thousand. Doesn't say much about her except she was born in California."

"I don't think the shooter was talking about someone who may be twenty-two and lives in California, too remote."

"There's another Estrada who plays baseball for the San Francisco Giants."

"Again, too remote."

"This is interesting," commented Dakota. "Estrada is sometimes used as the word ROAD in Spanish."

Wilt had written the clue down on a piece of paper while talking to Courts. "Let's take another look at the clue and exactly what it says." He picked up the paper and re-read the clue. "***The youngest daughter of Estrada was disappointed***. That doesn't sound like a road clue. It must be a well-known human. How many daughters did Alonso Estrade have?"

Dakota flipped through some computer pages and said, "Two. If the clue is about Beatriz the clue writer has bad grammar."

I think we have solved the clue, but not where the shooter is going to be. If we are correct the one obvious spot is at the Coronado Historical Site in Bernalillo."

"Why is the historical site located in Bernalillo?" asked Dakota.

"Because Coronado camped in and or around Bernalillo during his drive to find the cities of gold."

"That was in 1541, How do they know that?"

"Coronado brought with him on his quest about four hundred Europeans, two thousand Indians, a bunch of family members with servants, some slaves and dozens of pigs and cows for food. He spread artifacts all over the place, particularly where he camped. All around Bernalillo the historians dug up things that proved to belong to Coronado's army of explorers."

"Interesting. What's at the historical site?"

"The National Park Service has dug up remnants of an ancient pueblo. You can take a tour of where things were years and years ago. They offer a movie that explains the history of the area and what happened when Coronado and his troops invaded the area. They also have a real Kiva unearthed that you can enter and see the painting in the rounded, underground religious chamber."

"Kiva? What was it used for?"

"It was a chamber generally round that was used by the male members of the Pueblo for religious rites. As far as I know it is the only Kiva that you can enter. All other Kivas in the nineteen Pueblos in New Mexico are off limits to anyone other than those who live in the Pueblo. It's quite an experience. They also have an office where the history of the Pueblo people is displayed on one side of the office, along with Coronado's march into New Mexico with artifacts and historical articles. Outside you can see actual pictures that were taken off the walls of the Kiva that were painted hundreds of years ago. And, of course, they have a gift shop."

"I'll have to take some time and go through the site. It will further my education about the area."

Wilt said, "Another very interesting exhibit to see is at the Indian Pueblo Cultural Center. There they have the complete history of the Pueblos and various other exhibits. They also have Indian dances about every weekend, and a good Indian Pueblo Kitchen restaurant that serves Indigenous cuisine."

"Sounds like I have a lot to see and read to catch up with you."

"I'd be happy to take you around to these places when we are not trying to catch the bad guys."

Wilt noticed that Dakoda blushed, turned her head away and said, "I'll think about that." *I really don't know what I think but I don't want to discourage him* "But at first thought it sounds like a nice idea."

The phone rang and Wilt, reluctantly taking his eyes off Dakota, pressed the answer button and said, "Yes, Frank."

"We think we've solved the clue."

"We think we've solved it also," responded Wilt,.

"It has to do with Coronado and his trek through New Mexico."

"We agree," said Wilt.

Frank continued, "As you know, they camped up here close to Santa Fe which means the shooter is going for some politician who will be in the capital building."

When history says that Coronado camped close to Santa Fe, they say Santa Fe because the world has never heard of Bernalillo where they really camped. Wilt hesitated, and said, "Are you sure the shooter will not be after someone at the Coronado Historical Society complex?"

"What? No. That would be a complete gamble as to who is going to visit that facility. It is known which politicians will be at the capitol building. The shooter will go for one of them."

"But the legislature is out this time of year. They are only in session one or two months of the year in late January and early February. Two months for odd years and one month for even years."

"I know that Wilt. The governor has called a special session, and they will all be up in Sant Fe next week for a few days. That's the time the shooter will try for his target."

"I'll tell you what, Frank. You take your people up to Santa Fe and guard the capital building, and Dakota and I will go over to the historical site area and guard that area."

"The captain wants everyone to be around the capital building. I know you may not want to be there, but you are being paid by the police so I would expect you and Dakota to be with us in Santa Fe starting next week."

Shit! "I'll see you there Monday," Wilt said and clicked off.

CHAPTER TWELVE

Helcom figured the police would get the clue without much trouble. Once deciphered they would surround the Coronado Historical Site looking for the shooter and for the pick-up that the shooter drives. *I've got the SUV now and that should be worth at least two shots. Plus, will be easier to make my exit with the SUV. I know that the individual I'm looking for will be at the historical site because he couldn't stay away. He doesn't know I spent four hours on the computer last night looking for him. First I searched all the police I could find, to no avail. After that I searched retired police. It wasn't until I got through most of the private investigators that I found Mr. Morrison. There he was in all his glory, talking about his exploits and how he managed to complete sniper school in the Marine Corps. That's why he's snooping around where I may be shooting. OK, what I will do is shoot him. One more feather in my cap to show those bastards that I can be a military sniper.*

When the day arrived Helcom loaded her SUV with the necessary equipment and drove north along I-25 until she reached the turnoff for Bernalillo. She turned west off I-25 and continued through Bernalillo to the edge of the Rio Grande river. She knew there was a dirt road going north that followed the river. It was a popular area for exercise to walk along the river or canal. There would be several cars and trucks parked along the side of the road and she didn't think hers would be noticed.

There was a spot along the dirt road that came close to the river. Just across the river was the headquarters of the Coronado Historical Society. Helcom walked from the road, through the bushes to the river until she had a good view of the buildings on the other side. She estimated two hundred yards to the entrance of the office, and she figured that is where Morrison must go to warn the people there. As she went back to the SUV to get her gear she knew the firing of the shot would cause a hell of a racket. She hoped the water and bushes would cause enough of an echo that people would be confused for at least three to four minutes. That would give her time to get back in the SUV and drive out of the area. She knew the police would be looking for a pick-up which should give her time to escape. It would be close, but if she pulled it off it would be a very big feather in her bonnet. No one could deny that she was worthy of being a sniper.

She reached her SUV and retrieved her gear. She walked back and set up the rifle, calibrated the scope, got in a comfortable position, and waited. *He will be here shortly, I'm sure. Let's hope I can get out of this event after I hit the target.*

* * *

After talking to Frank about where the shooter was going to be, Wilt told Dakota he would meet her at the office at nine in the morning. He was thinking about stopping by the Coronado Historical Site tomorrow morning and talking to the rangers on duty there.

"I should probably at least warn them that a shooter may be in the area," he told Dakota.

"What will they do about it? They can't close the doors on a 'might be."

"No, but if they know there is a possibility of someone being shot they can request the visitors not to stand around the front door. They can also tell the guides to walk quickly between areas of interest. A shooter needs a few seconds to sight in, focus the scope, and let the air out of their lungs before starting to squeeze the trigger. If the target is moving it is much harder to hit."

"OK, I'll see you in the morning at nine o'clock," Dakota said as she turned toward the door.

Wilt watched her leave, stood at the window, and saw her cross the street as she walked toward her parked car. *She is really a nice-looking woman. She is also smart and catches on quickly. I like working with her.*

His train of thought was broken when his phone rang. He looked at it and saw that Georgie was calling.

"Hi Georgie."

"Hey there detective, coming over for dinner tonight? I'm fixing something special, chicken parmesan.

I'm kind of tired, Wilt thought, *but I can't disappoint her again.* I'm looking forward to it. I'll be there at five sharp."

"Don't plan on leaving early, dear. After dinner is just as important as dinner."

"Ok."

Wilt went home and took a shower, put on some clean clothes, and went over to Georgie's place for dinner. They both had a glass of wine before dinner and the discussion was not entirely comfortable. Georgie was concerned about their relationship.

"You just don't seem to be yourself lately Wilt. What's wrong?"

"Nothing's wrong Georgie. I'm constantly thinking about this killer that we're trying to catch. In fact, Dakota and I are going to Santa Fe tomorrow morning to start a visual watch for the shooter."

"You used to make love to me two or three times before we were finished. Now it's one and done. Something is not right. Your mind is too much on your work, or your partner, which is it?"

"My mind is on both. I need to watch Dakota because she is inexperienced, and I don't want her to make a mistake that will get her killed. I consider her my responsibility."

"That's nice Wilt," Georgie said. "But I don't want her to ruin our relationship. I still think you should move in with me so we can talk these things out. I think you are spending too much time around her."

Wilt felt his heart rate increase as he was getting a little annoyed. *Calm down Wilt, don't make this any worse than it is. Try and see Georgie's point.* "Maybe you're right. Once this shooter is found or compromised I will give it some real thought. I don't want to move in too soon after Pearl's death, and I don't want to be considered a "kept" man."

"I just heard the dinner bell go off. Let's go to the table and I'll serve dinner."

Saved by the bell. Now, why did I just think that? If the truth be known I don't want to move in with George because it would be very difficult if I ever wanted to move out. "OK, I'll pour the wine."

After dinner there was no more discussion about moving in or out. Their love making was better as Wilt lasted more than once and Georgie was happy. Wilt left her house around ten-thirty and went home and went to bed. His head was filled with images of Dakota, and he had a hard time going to sleep. The next morning, he went to the office and picked up Dakota.

"You look rested," she commented. "Get a good night's sleep?"

"Uh, yes I did. I didn't think much about our shooter and didn't take any sleeping pills. Might take me longer to go to sleep, but it seems I'm more rested in the morning."

"Are you still thinking about stopping by the historical site and talking to the rangers?"

"Yes, and I have another thought. I think if I were setting up a sniper shot at the building in front of the site, I would set up on the other side of the river. There are lots of bushes to hide behind and being seen would not be a problem."

"So, what are you going to do? Walk through the bushes looking for the shooter?" asked Dakota kind of sarcastically.

"No, I'm, or I should say we, are going to drive down the dirt road that follows the river on the opposite side of the site and look for a woman in a pick-up."

"Now that's the most logical thing you have said all morning,."

CHAPTER THIRTEEN

Helcom just knew Morrison would come by the historical site this morning. She also felt he would tell the rangers not to let people stand idly by the front door, and to walk quickly between exhibits. So, she made sure her scope was set and focused on the front door of the site. She noticed a Pueblo woman setting up a table where she would put her hand made jewelry for sale. Some other people were starting to arrive to take the first tour. *Morison better get his ass here and warn these people before I lose my patience and shoot somebody else.* After another ten minutes she saw Morrison walk up the three steps and enter the headquarters. The woman who she saw down at the Billy the Kid grave site was with him and followed him inside. Helcom waited for Morrison to exit the building and she would be ready to take her shot. Fifteen minutes later the door opened and the woman with Morrison walked out, with Morrison behind her. The woman kept walking, but Morrison stopped along the path, and looked in Helcom's direction. *Damn, it looks like he's looking directly at me. No, he can't see me among these bushes.* She refocused her scope from the front door to the target's head, put the cross hairs right on Morrison's forehead, exhaled, and slowly started to squeeze the trigger. BLAM!

* * *

Wilt and Dakota arrived at the Coronado Historical Site just as the rangers were opening the door to the headquarters building. It was the only building on the grounds and was in a U shape with the movie room and gift shop on one side, and the original paintings from the Kiva on the other. The rangers occupied the center portion, welcomed people, and set up the tours. There was also a secretary who collected the money for the tours. There was a back door which was used to start the tours. The back faced the former pueblo site, and two hundred yards further was the Santa Ana golf course. Wilt knew the most logical place for a shooter to set up was across the river to the East because of the lack of cover everywhere else.

Wilt parked the car and took a good look around the area from the parking place. Dakota exited the car and came around and stood by Wilt.

"What are you looking for? Can't see much from here."

"Wilt looked at Dakota's dark eyes and thought, *Maybe I'm crazy to stop here because I'm pretty sure the shooter is across the river waiting for a target. It could be a ranger, or a tourist, or maybe even me, or Dakota. Should I ask her to stay in the car while I go and talk to the rangers? She probably would not stay anyway.*

Dakota looked at Wilt and said a little louder, "What are you looking for?"

"I'm just thinking about the mind of the shooter. Do you want to stay in the car while I go and talk to them?"

"Wilt, I'm not a child, I'm a member of the Albuquerque Police Department. Maybe you should wait in the car while I go talk to them!"

"OK, I knew that would be your answer, but I had to try. I just don't want anything to happen to you. I'm kind of liking having you around."

I kind of like being around. "I'll be careful. Let's go because you know they will be waiting for us in Santa Fe."

They walked up the path to the headquarters building and entered. There were two rangers in the building, plus the secretary. Before the rangers said anything Wilt pulled out his credentials and told them who he was, he introduced Dakota, who showed her badge.

"You gentlemen, and lady, have been reading about the sniper or shooter that has been killing people around New Mexico?" asked Wilt.

The three of them nodded their heads in the positive.

"Well, we have reason to believe this area may be the next target and it could be sometime today," said Dakota.

The two rangers looked at each other. One said, "How strong is the evidence that you think it may be here and today?"

Ranger number two asked, without waiting for an answer from number one, "Why the hell would someone target this area?"

"I can't tell you how we came to suspect this area, but there is strong suspicion that the target is either here or at the capitol building in Sant Fe," Dakota added.

"Ok, what do you want us to do? Is the evidence strong enough for us to shut down?"

Wilt took a deep breath, "We don't think you need to shut down if you keep people from standing around the front door and walk quickly between exhibits. The shooter, if he or she is here, will concentrate on the area in front of the building."

"How do you know that?" one ranger asked.

"I was a sniper in the Marine Corps, and I know how the shooter will think. I looked at the cover in this area and the most logical shooting site is across the Rio Grande in the bushes. He has excellent cover, and a clear shot. If you look around the rest of the area there isn't a good place to shoot from."

"Ok. Marge," the first ranger said to the secretary, "I want you to go home. We can handle any money that needs to be taken, and Dick and I can also handle the tours. Once you get home would you call the two tour guides that are scheduled to work today and tell them not to come in? Tell them we'll explain later. I'll call Doris and tell her not to open the gift shop today. That should take care of it."

Marge said, "What about Little Eagle in the front of the building trying to sell her jewelry?"

"We'll move her to the back door. People can go out back to look at her trinkets. That will also act to keep them out in front."

Dakota said, "We appreciate your cooperation and do hope we're wrong."

"We'll manage. There's nothing special going on today so it should be rather quiet."

"We will be on our way. We need to get to Santa Fe in case we are wrong," Wilt said as he started toward the door. He motioned Dakota to go before him and said, "Move rather quickly please."

He opened the door, and she went out and started along the path toward the truck. As she was walking she turned to see Wilt standing on the path staring at something across the river.

Wilt was thinking. *If she's there she is now insuring the focus on the scope. Now she's aiming and letting out her breath. Now she's starting to squeeze on the trigger. It's time to move NOW!* He dropped to the ground just as the bullet missed his head and logged in one of the adobe bricks behind him. The sound of the shot echoed throughout the area.

"Wilt are you all right?" yelled Dakota as she ran toward him. She reached him just as he was getting up.

"Yes, I'm OK." He said as he brushed the dirt off his trousers. "Now we know where she is so let's see if everyone in the house is OK, after that let's get on that dirt road to find the pick-up."

A ranger came out of the headquarters and ran down to where Wilt and Dakota were standing. "Shouldn't we take cover?"

Wilt looked at him, "No, the shooter is getting out of the area. It's too open to hide from people walking along the road, and with that rifle noise, walkers will be curious. Everyone OK in the house?"

"Scared the shit out of us, but we're fine."

"I think you can go back to normal operations now. The shooter missed her, uh his target and is gone. We need to get out of here also to see if we can catch him."

The ranger looked at him, "You knew he was over there didn't you?"

"I was pretty sure, but I had to find out."

The ranger turned and started walking back to the headquarters building.

They started walking toward the SUV. "You could have been killed. You ducked just a fraction of a moment before she shot at you," said Dakota with a frown on her face.

"It really wasn't a gamble, Dakota. I made an educated guess. I figured her scope was set at the door of the entrance and if I stopped on the path she would have to re-focus. She would aim, let out her breath and squeeze the trigger. I figured if she was there and if I was the target I would have nine seconds from the time I stopped before I needed to hit the ground. I counted in my head, and I was correct."

"You came within a half a second of having your head blown off. Is it worth that?" said Dakota rather forcefully.

"Look what we have. We now know I'm a target which helps me get into her head and next time try to be at her waiting area before she is. We also will know the caliper of the gun as soon as we dig the bullet out of the adobe brick. I think it was worth the risk."

"Well, I don't," said Dakota as she turned around and headed toward the SUV. She didn't want Wilt to see the tear running down her cheek. "Come on we're wasting time."

* * *

Son-of-a -bitch, Helcom said under her breath. *I missed again. This time he acted like he knew I was going to shoot him, and he knew when to duck, just in time.* She suddenly realized she was still lying in the bushes. *I have to get the hell out of here. My plan is to quickly pack the SUV and rather than drive out to the main road, I'll drive further into the Bosque. They will be looking for someone in a pick-up driving fast trying to get out before the police come. I'm surprised there were no police at the historic site. Just Morrison and his side kick.*

Helcom quickly put her equipment in their cases and covered them in the back of the SUV. She put on a cowboy hat and pulled it down close to her ears. She put her hair up under the hat and donned a fake mustache. She was sure if anyone saw her they would think the driver was a man. She got in her SUV and headed north along the river. Her objective was to travel next to the river until she reached Algodones, take the I-25 south back to Albuquerque. She wanted the police to think a woman driving a pick-up had pulled off the road somewhere near the river and hid her truck. No one along the road would have seen her.

In order to check her plan, she pulled up next to a couple walking along the road and in a deep voice asked, "Did either of you hear a gun shot a short while ago?"

"The woman responded, "Yes we heard it. Do you know what it was?"

"Probably someone hunting out of season," Helcom said. "No big deal. See you later." She pushed on the gas pedal and drove off.

She knew the speed limit for non-posted county roads in New Mexico was fifty-five miles per hour. It used to be seventy-five mph just the same as Interstate Highways, but the law was changed a few years ago. The State Legislature figured dirt roads were not built for that kind of speed, so it was changed to fifty-five. *Fifty-five is plenty fast for a dirt road. I'm going to go through the Santa Ana Reservation, so I need to watch for posted speeds. Don't want to get a ticket with all this gear.* She also knew that it is illegal for anyone to have a firearm on an Indian Reservation. Each reservation had its own police force. It didn't matter if you had a concealed weapons permit, it was still illegal. *Most of these reservation police will not search the car unless they have a pretty good reason. A lot of them are retired state or city police officers and they don't hassle you too much. It is also bad for business if the reservation has a casino.*

* * *

Wilt was driving slower than he wanted to, but he and Dakota were watching for places a pick-up could be hidden and not be seen from the main road. They had come across a few couples walking along the road and stopped to question them. No one had seen a woman driving a pick-up and almost all had heard the gun shot. Most thought it was an illegal hunter, but no one had seen anyone hunting.

Wilt had called Frank Courts and told him that the shooter was not in Santa Fe. Frank asked how Wilt knew, and Wilt told him about being shot at.

"You mean to tell me you stood there and let this guy take a shot at you? Are you nuts or what?" said Frank when Wilt told him what he had done.

"It was a calculated risk. I didn't think I was in much danger. But we are now driving north on the river road, and no one had seen a woman in a pick-up. It's like she just disappeared."

"The river is pretty low, maybe she drove across it someplace."

"Not likely because there is no road on the other side and she would have to drive through a couple of golf courses, or soccer fields, or in and out of canyons."

"You know if she kept on going north she could come out on I-twenty-five at Algodones which is ten miles from Bernalillo, where you got on the river road."

Wilt said, "I thought about that, but no one has seen a pick-up going that direction."

Dakota was listening to the conversation. "If no one has seen a pick-up, and we have not discovered a place she could hide it, maybe she's not driving a pick-up anymore. How about asking if anyone has seen a woman driving a vehicle down this road today. Forget the pick-up."

Both Wilt and Frank thought that was a very good idea.

Dakota continued, "Let's think a minute. She has had time to do something with the pick-up. We checked all the used tire dealers in

Albuquerque and Santa Fe and no woman turned in tires for newer ones. She could have gone to Las Cruses or even El Paso to buy tires, or even change cars. Who knows what she's driving now?"

Frank added: "Start asking people if they saw a woman driving the road. If so, what kind of car? It has to be rather large because she has to have a place to put her equipment. Meanwhile I'll call off the watch crew in Santa Fe. I hate to say this Wilt, but you were right once again."

"We'll start asking right away," answered Wilt. He clicked off his phone and looked at Dakota. "Good thinking Miss Chavez."

Dakota smiled as Wilt started driving along the road once again. This time they were looking for people walking along, not a pick-up. After stopping four couples and two singles with no results, one couple said they did see a strange person driving a SUZ going north.

"He stopped and asked me if we heard the gun shot," said the female walker. "He had a funny looking mustache and a strange voice. I told my boyfriend I thought it was a woman in disguise."

"What was she driving?"

"An SUV," the male partner said.

"Color? License number? Age?" Dakota asked.

"I don't know the age, but it wasn't new. The color was kind of gray, and I didn't pay any attention to the license plate number.

"Did you notice if the vehicle had a license plate on the front?" she continued.

"No, I didn't notice. The only thing I did notice was on the rear it had a Texas license plate.

"It had a Texas license? That's important," Wilt said.

Wilt thanked them and drove on. "A Texas plate tells me that she bought the car in El Paso. Probably traded in her pick-up. So, all we have to do is check all the places she could have bought the car."

"What's the population of El Paso?" asked Dakota as she was pulling out her cell phone. "Says here it's almost seven hundred thousand."

"How many places have used cars?" asked Wilt as he drove along.

Dakota worked on her cell phone. "Looks like at least thirty places, not counting new car sales where they would each probably have used cars. It also does not include all the people who are selling their car, or trying to trade it in. This is not going to be a ten-minute job to check all these places. Who knows if the individual you are talking to will tell you the truth?"

"We'll see if Frank and the APD have the resources to do the search."

"What do you expect to find?" asked Dakota. "After all that canvasing we find out that some woman bought an SUV and traded in a pick-up, probably paid cash. Don't we know it was her that shot at you? Sounds like a lot of work to find what we already know.?

"Maybe we can get some DNA off the pick-up which may lead us to a name.

He stopped three other couples walking along and all had seen a gray SUV but didn't have any other information. As they kept going north the road started following a canal rather than the road.

"Well, we missed her. She's gone by now. She's smarter than I thought if she changed vehicles," Wilt said.

"She's clever enough to keep at least one step ahead of us. Changing cars was smart, so was putting on a disguise after taking the shot.

She knew someone would be asking about a female and pick-up," lamented Dakota.

"She also knows we are closer to her now than before. It would not surprise me if she stopped giving clues. Or at least made them more complicated. Let's go back to the historical grounds and dig that bullet out of the adobe brick."

CHAPTER FOURTEEN

When Helcom hit the I-25 freeway south of Santa Fe, she knew she had once again avoided capture. *That was a little too close. I better be more careful and stick to places with several escape routes. My clues need to be more general because of Morrison. He thinks he knows how I think, and maybe he does.*

The next day when Helcom was working at the shooting range, She was listening to three men discussing what they were going to do the upcoming weekend. One of the men talked about driving up to Jemez Springs area with his new girlfriend.

"It's a great drive on Friday and it will be a beautiful day. I'm looking forward to driving the whole circle, from Jemez Springs through Los Alamos and on to Santa Fe and home with my girlfriend."

"Girlfriend? I thought you were married," asked one of the three men.

"I am," the first man said as he and his friends started to walk out of the door. "I'm getting tired of the old lady, and I need some new meat."

You are my next target, asshole. Thought Helcom. *I'll follow you home and find what kind of car you drive and where you live. On Friday I'll wait for you somewhere behind a rock and you will die.*

She took stock of the individual as he walked to his black pickup. He was fairly large and wore a cowboy hat and cowboy boots. As he entered his truck he stuck an unlit cigar in his mouth. He put the truck in reverse and Helcom looked at the front of his truck. She saw he had a front plate with a New Mexico flag displayed. Once again she followed him to his house and took a picture of him and his truck. She was convinced she would recognize it on the road after Jemez Springs.

She started thinking about the next clue. *First I must pick a place, examine it for access roads, or I could change my method of operation. I could see what the possibility would be if I didn't try and run away. What if I pitched a tent near the shooting area and camped, pretending I had been there a couple of days? No, the police would find me and take me in for questioning. Let's see, what if I walked a mile away from where I parked the car and climbed a tree and shot from there. I could stay up the tree until the search was over. That's a stupid thought? I need a place where I can shoot from that no one can reach for at least twenty minutes. The top of a mountain shooting down on a road, for example. I may be able to find a place in the area around Jemez Springs in the high mountains. I need to take a ride tomorrow up that way and find a spot where I could see the coming traffic for at least a quarter mile. The police would think it was a random target because very few people would be that area. My clue could be interesting also.*

The next morning Helcom took the trip she was thinking about. According to the map of the area, the road she was on took a sharp curve just outside of the only town in the area. As the road straightened out it also increased in altitude. Just before the curve she could see the road down the hill where she had come from. Helcom stopped the car and walked across the road to look at the view. There was a good line of sight on the lower section of the road, and she knew she could shoot through the windshield of a car coming up the road.

I've got my shooting spot now. My next action is to find a place to park the vehicle where it is difficult to see from the road where I am. This problem was solved in a short time, so she was now ready to send in the clue.

* * *

Wilt and Dakota drove back to the office after digging the bullet out of the adobe brick.

"Looks like a three-Oh-eight. We'll take it back and give it to Franke so he can have it verified. Now we can start looking for people who are buying this caliber ammo. I know it will be a long shot, but we don't have a lot to go on."

"I would not play with the shooter anymore, like you did this morning," said Dakota.

"Maybe it was kind of stupid, but this person is going around killing people and we need to stop her."

"There has to be a better way than that. I'm just getting used to you,' said Dakota as she turned her head away from his view.

"I too am just getting used to you Dakota, and I'm impressed with what I see and observe. You think well, are decisive, not afraid to speak up, and I have to say it, very nice looking."

Dakota blushed a little. "Thank you. Now, where were we?"

"I'm about to go over for dinner at Georgie's house. She's getting upset because I'm spending so much time on this case. Some of it may be my time I'm spending with you."

"Well, I'm part of the group assigned to this case. You have to spend time with me if you want to work on the case. Want me to talk to her?"

"No, I'll work it out. I'm sure everything will be fine. I'll see you in the morning. Maybe we can figure out where the next shot will come from. It has to be someplace well known, good escape routes and accessible."

"Sounds like downtown Albuquerque," remarked Dakota with a smile.

Wilt locked the office, stopped by the police station, and gave Frank the smashed bullet.

"I think it's a three-o-eight" said Wilt.

"OK, we'll have the lab verify that. Dumb way to get a sample bullet."

"I know, but at least we have something we didn't have before."

Wilt went back to his car and started toward Georgie's large house. He thought about what he was going to say and tried to imagine her response. He anticipated a difficult conversation and her getting angry. *I don't know how I can soft peddle this. The truth is the pleasure of my visits is getting less and less. If I tell her that all hell will break loose. I'll stick to my story that most of my time is taken up with this assignment.*

He kept thinking about the anticipated response to his conversation. When he drove into the garage Georgie came out of the kitchen and met him.

She gave him a hug and said, "It's nice to finally see you Wilt. I know, lots of time needs to be spent on the job."

Wilt hesitated, "We need to discuss this problem, Georgie. I think it might be best if I just stayed at my condo for a while. It's faster to get to the office from my condo and since I'm spending so much time on the job, it would be easier on me." *OK, here it comes!*

Georgie looked at him, her eyes teared up, and she said, "Goodbye Wilt." She turned around and went back into the house.

Well, shit. That went better than I thought, but now I feel like a jerk.

Wilt drove back to his condo and went to bed. He didn't sleep much that night wondering if he'd made a mistake with Georgie. *Time will tell. Now I can concentrate more on the job, and Dakota.*

The next morning when Wilt arrived at the office Dakota was already there.

"How did your talk go with Georgie last evening?" She asked.

"I'm not really sure," he replied. "When I told her I need to spend more time at my condo because it's closer to the office, she said "Goodbye" and walked back in the house."

"Was this after dinner?"

"No, it was right when I got there. I suspect we are no longer an item, but I'm not positive. I expected her to put up some objections, but she didn't. Just said goodbye and left."

"How do you feel about it?' asked Dakota.

"To tell you the truth I feel like I just stepped out of concrete. I was constantly worried about how she was going to act every day these last two weeks. It wore me down. I'm relieved I can concentrate on the job."

"Doesn't sound like a healthy relationship, but it really isn't any of my business."

Wilt looked at her, "It kind of is your business because if I can't concentrate it may affect my thinking and that could be dangerous for me or both of us."

"Yeah, like taking a sniper's bullet in the forehead?"

"OK, let's forget about that and think about the next clue, if one comes in. In the meantime, do you want to go to the Albuquerque rifle range and do a little practice shooting?"

"Yes I would like that. I have not shot a sniper's distance, just pistol shooting. What is the maximum distance at the Albuquerque Shooting Range Park?"

"It's not the general sniper's range but you can get steel targets out at seven hundred and fifty yards. It's a hundred and thirty yards from being a half mile."

"My shooting gear is in my apartment. It will take me probably an hour to get it and be back here ready to go."

"That's a good idea. We will leave it in the office after the shoot so it will be handy if we need it."

"See you soon." And Dakota walked out the door.

CHAPTER FIFTEEN

Wilt and Dakota walked into the office at the shooting range. They paid for two shooting spots and went out and drove to the range. They waited until **all clear** was given before storing their gear at their shooting station, walked out to look at their steel targets to see if they could tell where they hit once they completed their round. Once back at their stations they readied their weapons, put on their ear and eye protection, and held their rifles ready to load. Once the signal was given to get ready they loaded their rifles. Another signal was given, and they took the prone position and sighted in at the targets. They proceeded to shoot. Wilt shot six shots and Dakota shot five shots before the **All Stop** was signaled. Once again they walked out to the targets and marked where the bullets hit. All of the shots for both individuals were in the darkened bullseye center section. Two of Dakota's bullets broke the paint on the side of the bullseye, but all of Wilt's were close to dead center.

"Nice shooting," said Wilt. "You certainly know how to handle your weapon. I'd take those shots any day."

"Thanks," Dakota said, a little disappointed that she didn't do better.

They shot four more sessions and Dakota did as well as Wilt in the final two shootings.

As they were storing their gear in Wilt's SUV, Dakota said, "That was nice, I enjoyed it. I haven't had a chance to shoot much long range since I was hired as a police officer. Mostly our shooting was with pistols."

"Let's go into the office and see which day is the least busy. Maybe we can set up some kind of regular morning practice time once we explain who we are and why we need to practice."

They walked into the office and found the regular clerk had already left for home. His replacement was a short, stocky female who greeted them.

"Can I help you?"

"My name is Wilt Morrison, and this is Dakota Chavez. I'm a private investigator and this is my assistant. We'd like to practice our shooting the same time each week if it's possible?"

The person behind the counter said, "I'm sorry but we cannot make reservations for anyone. It's the course policy."

"But we're on police business," replied Wilt. "That should allow some kind of preference."

"What kind of police business?" asked the lady behind the counter.

"I'm a policeman," replied Dakota, "and we're after the person that is shooting up the area."

Wilt looked at Dakota and slightly shook his head in the negative.

"I don't know if that matters," replied the counter lady.

"Well, what about just reserving a station or two because we will be shooting at the steel targets," asked Dakota.

"Why are you shooting at the steel targets. Are you some kind of sniper?" asked the counter person.

Dakota didn't say anything as she suddenly thought maybe she'd said too much already.

"Those steel targets are almost always available if you come out here first thing when we open. Call before you come and ask the range manager if they are open. That's the best I can do."

"Ok thank you," said Wilt. As they neared the door, Wilt turned around and asked the counter girl her name.

"My name is Helcom Garcia," she said. *I know who you are, what you look like and who your assistant is. This is going to be easy.*

* * *

After putting up their shooting gear they both went back to Wilt's office. Wilt didn't say anything to Dakota about what she said to the counter lady. He thought she already knew she should not have said anything about their mission.

Dakota brought up the subject, "Sorry I opened my big mouth," she said.

"I think you learned something back there and realize the danger of telling someone our mission. You don't know who she is and who she knows, or who she talks to."

"I know. I'm sorry."

Wilt's phone rang and it was Frank Courts calling. "Enough about that." Wilt said as he put the phone on speaker.

"We received another clue," Courts said. "It may be a little more difficult. The clue is **Death under the old man's nose.**" So, you two discuss it and see what you come up with. I figure we only have a few days before the so-called sniper strikes again."

Dakota was the first to speak after Wilt clicked off the phone. "A guess all we have to do is find the right statue or displayed figure and we have the answer."

"That may be the case, but if you start looking there are several statues of old men around New Mexico. One that comes to mind immediately is the statue of Zozobra."

"Who?" asked Dakota.

"Each year in September the city of Santa Fe hosts the Fiesta De Santa Fe, which celebrates the coming of Diego De Vargas into the city. He arrived in the city in 1692 and brought Spanish dominion back to New Mexico. If you recall the Pueblo Revolt was in 1680 so De Vargas was the first Conquistador to return to New Mexico after the revolt. The Spanish left the Pueblo Indians alone for twelve years before returning. A whole procession of men dressed up like Diego De Vargas and his troops march into Santa Fe for the start of the celebrations."

"I'm surprised they can get away with that parade based on today's feelings about the past," said Dakota.

'In fact, there have been major protests by indigenous people about the march into the city. They maintain Diego De Vargas was better than most Spaniards who conquered New Mexico but was still mean to the Pueblo people. The march into Santa Fe may be changed in the future. Anyway, to start the Fiesta a fifty-foot marionette effigy called Zozobra is built out of wood, cloth, and straw. This figure represents the feelings of gloom and sadness, so it is burned to start the Fiesta De Santa Fe. Last year I think over sixty thousand people attended the event.."

"I assume this effigy has a big nose?" said Dakota.

"Yep, a very big nose. But the event is in September and we're sitting here in late July, so I don't think that's what she's referring to. There are other statues of old men around."

"It has to be large enough for a target to get under, at least that's what I get out of the clue."

Wilt thought for a moment, "You're probably right. Let's do some research about statues in New Mexico and see what we can fine."

Wilt started to look for statues of old men, and Dakota started to phone gun stores to see if she could find names of individuals who purchased 306 ammunition. After two hours they got together to compare what they had found.

Wilt went first, "I found a couple of statues of Coronado on a horse and some other statues but none that meet the criteria. There is one possibility in Clovis, New Mexico. *The Clovis Man* is a statue on the community college campus depicting the earliest documented Americans who lived in that area about eleven thousand years ago. It shows a cave -type man pulling a spear out of a Mammoth's head."

"Where's Clovis?" asked Dakota.

"Way east, right on the New Mexico and Texas border.

"And they documented that Americans lived there eleven thousand years ago?"

"Yes, by the artifacts they found while digging around the town. Most notable was the tip of spears. The tips were of a certain size and shape. They determined the age by using spectrometry. To celebrate this discovery, they put up the aforementioned statue of a man killing a Mammoth."

"Can someone get under his nose?" asked Dakota.

"Probably not," responded Wilt. "Other than that, I've struck out."

"I didn't do much better. I called eighteen-gun stores in Albuquerque and Rio Rancho and half told me they hadn't sold any three-oh-eight ammo in a few weeks, and the other half told me to get a subpoena and come down to the store before they would disclose any information about their customers.

"That doesn't surprise me. We need to start re-thinking this latest clue. What besides statues can someone get under a nose?"

Dakota thought a moment, "Could it be the shape of something? Something like a large rock, or a tree? Something that could represent a nose?"

"Once again good thinking, Dakota. If that's the case it opens up the whole state and a gazillion different possibilities. Let's go home and sleep on it. I'll check with Frank Courts in the morning. Maybe they have some ideas about what the clue is saying." Wilt looked at Dakota for a moment and said, "You want to go someplace and get a bite to eat?"

Dakota hesitated for a second, "I have some things I have to get done tonight. I'll take a rain check on that invitation."

"Fair enough," was Wilt's response, sounding a little disappointed.

They both went down to the parking lot, got in their cars, and left.

I'll keep trying, thought Wilt. *I'm getting to enjoy her company.*

When Wilt got home, his phone rang. He pulled it out of his pocket and read the name of the caller: "Georgie" it read. Wilt was surprised and almost didn't answer, but thought better of it and said, "Hello, Georgie."

"Wilt, I have missed you. I know how I acted the last time we were together, but I'd like to have you come for dinner tonight and we can discuss our relationship like a couple of adults. I'm asking you to please do that for me. We were close enough not to end our relationship without being friends."

Wilt hesitated for a moment, "Alright, I agree. Give me a half hour to clean up and change and I'll be over."

"Thank you," responded Georgie. They both said goodbye and clicked off. Wilt thought, *I really have mixed feelings about Georgie. I'm attracted to her, but she embarrasses me from time to time with her forwardness. Do I tell her that? Do I tell her that I'm getting feelings for Dakota? Hell, I really don't know what I'm going to tell her. I'll just play it by ear and see what happens.*

CHAPTER SIXTEEN

Helcom was sitting in the parking lot next to the office building where Wilt had his office. She watched them both exit the building and walk toward their cars in the same lot she was parked. She figured she was far enough away that they would not notice her. They separated and got in their individual vehicles. Helcom started her SUV and slowly drove out of the lot following Dakota at a three-car distance.

I need to see where she lives, thought Helcom. *If I can somehow make friends with her I can gleam information about where they think the sniper is going to appear. I just have to make sure I don't slip and give her the idea I'm the sniper. In that case I'll have to kill her, which may be a good idea eventually anyway.*

The two cars drove West for a few blocks, turned East on to Menaul Avenue toward the Sandia mountain. Drivers around the Albuquerque area always knew their directions because the 10,400-foot Sandia mountain was always to their east.

Following a safe distance behind her, Helcom also turned on Menaul. They kept going until Dakota reached Tramway Boulevard and turned north. After three miles she turned into an apartment complex, parked in a parking lot, and walked toward her room.

Helcom watched until Dakota turned a corner and went out of sight. Helcom quickly got out of the car and turned the same corner just in time to see Dakota unlock her apartment.

Room 320-C. I will remember that. In fact, I think my imaginary room will be 110-B. If she thinks I also live here it will be easier to get her to be friendly. Helcom walked around the complex until she found room 110-B. *Now I can explain where my room is and what kind of view I have. One more thing to do.* She walked toward the front of the building and found the office. She walked in and talked to the person behind the counter. She found that there are a few rentals available and the price for one bedroom was twelve hundred per month. *I can discuss the price, so I think I'm set. All I have to do is be very careful that she doesn't see me come and go at late hours. Time to get on the road and do my sniper's duty.*

Helcom returned to her apartment and got her gear ready for the next shot. Once the car was loaded she made dinner for herself, had some wine with dinner and went to bed.

* * *

Wilt pulled up in front of Georgie's house, got out and rang the bell. Georgie opened the door and gave Wilt a quick kiss on the cheek.

"Thank you for coming, as I said over the phone I have missed you."

"I basically missed you too, Georgie," Wilt said. "As you know the state sniper case has consumed me. I spend all of my time working and thinking about this damn shooter."

As they walked into the house toward the sitting room, Georgie said, "I know. I 'm not naive enough to think that's all that is occupying your time. I would appreciate us being truthful with each other, Wilt." She stopped and turned toward him, "I need to know exactly where I stand with you."

Wilt wasn't sure what to say. "I like working with Dakota. She's smart and makes good intelligent suggestions about what to do next. She's a good worker and does what I ask her to do without questioning my directions. But please understand, I have not touched her, nor have we had any discussion about any feelings between us."

Georgie poured two glasses of wine, gave one to Wilt, and sat down in a padded chair. "Your avoidance of me is more than your attention to the job. What happened between us?'"

"Georgie you are a great looking lady. You're smart, talented..."

"Wilt," she interrupted, "What is it about me you don't like? I'm not interested in what you do like because what you don't like is what is driving you away."

Wilt thought for a moment, "Georgie, the things I don't like, or make me feel uncomfortable around you, are the things that attracted me to you in the first place. Your style of sensual movement, your forward comments, and where you touch me and what you say to me in public sometimes make me uncomfortable."

"I can work to change that," she said.

"I can't ask you to change the things that make you the way you are. Those actions make you stand out from other women. It just takes someone that appreciates them because that's who you are. Trying to change your personality would make you miserable. You're Georgie Frost, the fun and outgoing female. Lots of men would give anything to have you on their arm, I'm just not one of them because I can't appreciate your style."

She took a deep breath and said, "I guess there is no reason you need to stay for dinner."

Wilt felt his heart pound harder in his chest. "Make no mistake, Georgie, I appreciate everything you've done for me. You helped Pearl and me when we needed to hide from people following us. You helped me through the grief I felt after Pearl's death. You helped me dispose of Pearls things. I will always be grateful, and I hope we can remain friends."

Georgie's eyes became tear coated and she turned her head away from Wilt. "I'll always have a soft spot in my heart for you Wilt. It's just that I can't be around you without wanting to walk up and give you a hug and a kiss. Maybe I'll get over that feeling, but I don't think so. Please leave now before I start crying."

Wilt got up and walked toward the door. He turned and said, "As you go through life you meet a lot of people. Some you remember and some you don't. The special ones leave footprints on your heart. Your footprints will always be on my heart. You are a fine individual Georgie, and I'm sorry it has to end this way. Good-bye." He turned and walked out the door. As he walked to his SUV he felt kind of empty and deflated.

He thought, *Maybe I'm crazy giving up that woman. She does have some great attributes and can afford to do anything and go anywhere. I just don't feel the things I need to feel. I need to feel anxious to be with her; a deep longing sensation to hold her and kiss her; wanting to protect her; worrying about her when I'm not here. Thinking about her when I wake up in the morning; thinking about her when I go to bed at night; getting seen with her; yes she's good in bed, but that's not the only thing that matters. My feelings for Georgie that are considered to be defined as love just aren't there. I wish they were.*

* * *

Helcom got up early the next morning, had some breakfast and drove out of her complex. She went north on I-25 and turned east on to Highway 550 toward Farmington. She drove past the Zia Pueblo and when she arrived at San Ysidro she turned right on to Highway 4. She drove for another twenty-six miles through some beautiful country before she stopped. She traveled up the curvy road and maneuvered the car into a brushy area and stopped. She retrieved her gear and walked across the street and up the hill, which was peppered with trees and brush. She found her objective, which was a view of the road she had just driven over which was down the hill from where she stood. Putting down the tripod, she pulled up some small brush to clear the way for her rifle. In a few minutes she was lying prone with her head high enough to see through her rifle scope. She put on her ear protection and her clear eyeglasses.

I'll wait until a white pickup comes along toward me going slow and get a nice shot into the windshield and into the forehead of the driver. This one is really going to surprise the people looking for the city sniper, especially Wilt, what's his name and his side kick. It will take them over an hour to get here and by that time I'll be in Santa Fe. Little do they know that the curvature of the road looks like an old man with a big nose. What a clever clue I gave them.

It wasn't long before she saw what she wanted. A large pick-up was moving slowly toward her on the road below, going the speed limit. The truck had two people in the front seat and no children were seen in the rear seats. Helcom looked in her scope, estimated the distance and speed of the truck, and pulled the trigger. She saw the bullet make a hole in the windshield and the truck slowly veer to the left side of the road and rolled off a small incline into the brush and stopped. She could hear screaming coming from the truck and knew it was from the passenger, which meant she had hit her target.

She grabbed her gear and walked down the hill and back to her SUV. She noticed that no vehicles were coming from either direction. She carefully put the rifle and tripod back in their respective boxes and covered them with a small carpet. She once again looked around for other vehicles and seeing none, removed a rake from the back of the SUV. She raked the tire marks from the road to the vehicle, got into the SUV. She had no trouble getting back on the road and once again stopped and raked the tire marks. She pointed the SUV north and headed for Santa Fe.

* * *

"We just received a report that someone shot the driver of a pickup north of Jemez Springs," Frank Courts told Wilt over the phone. Wilt was sitting in his office talking to Dakota about the clue that the shooter had left them when Frank called.

"We're on our way," Wilt said. He turned to Dakota and told her what Frank had said.

"Where is Jemez Springs?' said Dakota. "Are there statues of men with big noses in that area?"

"Bring your laptop along with your gear," he told Dakota. "I have an idea we'll find the nose on our way up there."

As they entered Interstate 25 and headed north, Wilt decided to brief Dakota on where they were going and the significance of some of the terrain.

"There are some significant sights and things that we are going to drive through on our way up to Jemez Springs," said Wilt, as he turned on to highway 550 going north. "First, we will go past the Zia Pueblo. The official sign for New Mexico is called the ZIA, which is known as the Sun Symbol. It has four lines protruding from the center circle. Each line represents the four main directions, the four seasons of the year, four phases of life and four periods of the day. The center circle represents the sun. The Zia people developed the Zia and gave it the Pueblo's name. In nineteen twenty-five the Daughters of the America Revolution held a design contest to choose a symbol that represented the State of New Mexico. The Zia was chosen and started being used on all kinds of things without the permission of the Zia Pueblo. As you would expect the Zia was a religious symbol for the Pueblo and they objected to its general use, but had no vote, so no power. The Zia is misused all over the state but is now recognized as the symbol of New Mexico."

"Does the Pueblo get anything for its use?" Dakota asked.

"It does get royalty from various organizations that ask permission and get approval to use the Zia. Apparently organizations just use it without asking and put all kinds of modifications to the symbol."

As they drove north Dakota noticed the terrain changing. It went from the Rio Grande Valley around Albuquerque to mountains, some with flat tops.

"Ahead is the village of San Ysidro. It was founded in 1899 by the King of Spain as a farming community. The population has dwindled to less than two hundred, but it is known as the gateway to the Jemez Mountains. We'll turn off on route number four and head for Jemez Springs. We'll drive through the Jemez Pueblo."

Dakota was struck by the beauty of the drive up through the mountains. After passing the Jemez Pueblo they came to Jemez

Springs. It looked like a little town with lots of buildings that housed artists and jewelry makers who selling their wares.

"Jemez Springs dates back at least five hundred years. Its name comes from the Jemez Pueblo and abundant nurturing hot springs. People come from miles around to stay and relax in the hot springs. The town is also known for one of its restaurant and saloons called Los Ojos, and it advertises it has been serving cowpokes, city folks, drifters, hikers, bikers, and debutantes since nineteen forty-seven. It has good food and a great atmosphere. Lots of people drive up from the Albuquerque area to have lunch or dinner at Los Ojos."

As Wilt was driving, paying attention to the speed limit, he asked Dakota to open her laptop and bring up a map of Jemez Springs. She complied and in a few minutes her screen filled with the surrounding terrain.

"Make the screen picture smaller," asked Wilt. "What we are looking for is where the curvature of the road doubles back on itself and makes an image of an old man."

Dakota did as she was asked and looked at the road, "Well yes, about five miles past Jemez Springs the road makes a large "U" curve and it kind of looks like an old man's head. And the head has a protruding nose."

"Damn," said Wilt. "I wish I had remembered that sooner. I used to come here with my family. I remember my dad remarking one time that the road looked like a man's head. That's where the shooter got the clue. I bet the person who was killed was driving north and when he came under the nose she shot him. What a waste of innocent life.

They continued on Route 4 through Jemez Springs and stopped when they saw the police cars on the road. It looked like a pickup truck had run off the left side of the road and was stuck in some of the brush growing along the road. Wilt and Dakota stopped and walked up to the police officer guarding the accident site. Dakota showed him her badge and Wilt explained who he was, and the guard let them though the tape.

Wilt noticed a young woman being consoled by a female police officer. He deduced it was the passenger who was trying not to cry. They looked inside of the cab and saw where the bullet went through the windshield. They also noted the blood and other carnage in the cab. The dead body was gone, and they found that the young lady who was being consoled was waiting for her parents to come and take her home. Wilt and Dakota walked back down the road to the location where the pickup was struck.

Wilt looked up the road, after that he looked up the hill to his right toward where the road curved and went the opposite direction. He said to Dakota, "She drove up the road to where she crossed over and could see the oncoming traffic. Calculating the speed and distance of the target would not be a problem. Once she fired she cleaned up the brush around her, walked back to her car and left. Let's see if we can go up and spot where she waited for her target to arrive. I guess she didn't have a problem with the noise of the rifle shot. Few people are up here this time of the year. About mid-summer it gets really crowded.

They got back in their car and drove up the road. Just before a curve Wilt stopped and looked back. He could see down the straight road where they had been. Wilt drove slowly so Dakota could watch the roadside for any marks or tracks. Wilt kept his eyes on the left side of the road.

"There are some tracks," he said as he noticed where a vehicle had driven off the right side of the road. He put on his blinkers and stopped. "She crossed the road and went up the hill on your side," he said to Dakota. "You see anything?"

"No," she responded as she exited the vehicle. Taking a closer look, she said, "I think I see some shoe or boot marks over here." As she started to follow the marks. The ground was hard, and the tracks were incomplete.

"Climb up the hill until you can see the road below us. You may find some disturbed bushes where she set up for the shot."

Dakota walked to where she could see the part of the road they had traveled and watched as police walked around the crime scene gathering information. *Somewhere around here the shooter must have planted the bipod and removed some of the brush in order to get a clear shot.* Walking in larger circles and being careful not to slip down the hill, Dakota finally saw some brush removed and thrown in a small pile. Picking up one of the bushes she noticed the stems of the bush was rough. *No chance to get a fingerprint off this stem. There are no smooth surfaces and at best only small portions of a finger touched each surface. The boot or shoe tracks have the same problem. The shooter either scuffed them on purpose, or she walked that way because of the heavy load she was carrying. Maybe she is crippled and scuffs her shoes when she walks.* Dakota looked for a cartridge but could not find one. She looked back at the crime scene and thought, *It was a good shot to hit that pickup driver as he was coming up the road. She's no slouch and knows her business.*

Wilt came through the brush and walked over to where Dakota stood. "Find anything useful?" he asked.

"Not really. Shoe prints are smeared, and the brush she touched have rough stems which will not hold a fingerprint. I also have not found a cartridge anywhere around where she fired her shot. Unless someone drove by and saw her going back to her car, we're out of luck."

"Did you find where she actually did the shooting? If she used a bipod on her rifle it may have left a mark on the ground. There are several different bipods that can be used, some of which have a distinctive profile at the end that rests in the dirt, or whatever the shooter is leaning on. See if we can find a mark."

They both started looking at the ground trying to find where a tripod mark might be located. After a few minutes Dakota thought she saw something that could be a bipod footprint.

"Over here Wilt, "she said as she was looking at the ground. "I may have something.

Wilt walked over and studies the ground marks. "Could be but it's pretty faint. I'll take a picture with my phone and maybe they can blow it up in the lab. It could be one more piece of evidence that we can put together which may help us overall." After taking the picture he said, "We didn't see her pass us on our way up here, so she kept going around to Santa Fe and back to Albuquerque. I guess we should follow the same trail, maybe we'll get lucky somewhere along the way."

They both walked back to Wilt's SUV and continued along Route 4. A few miles down the road they came to a large meadow-like area beside the road. Dakota was impressed with the expansion of the area in the middle of a forest.

Wilt noticed Dakota looking at the meadow. "You're looking at the Valles Caldera, which was formed over a million years ago.

It was formed by a super eruption under the ground followed by additional eruptions up until about forty thousand years ago. Valles Caldera, sometimes called the Jemez Caldera, is the oldest of three caldera-type volcanoes in the United States; the other two are Yellowstone and Long Valley in California. The caldera is a twelve by fourteen-mile depression. Lots of Elk and other animals roam here. Obviously, there is no hunting in the Caldera, but hiking and fishing are allowed."

"Never seen anything like it. Only in New Mexico, Land of Enchantment."

They continued on Route 4 until they came to Route 501, towards Los Alamos. Once again Wilt became the tour guide.

"I assume you have heard of Los Alamos?" he said.

"Yes," said Dakota. "That's where the Adam Bomb was developed with a consortium of scientists working on the Manhattan Project."

"There is a museum in town that shows the history of the area and the making of the bombs. Los Alamos probably has one of the highest rated high schools in the nation. There are numerous PhD's that work in the lab, and their smart kids go to the local schools. Plus, it also has one of the highest average income levels in the country."

They continued on state Route 502 and came to a sign that indicted Bandelier National Monument was straight ahead, and Los Alamos was to the left. Wilt stopped the car and sat there thinking. "I'm pretty sure she didn't go to Los Alamos this way. There is a military checkpoint you must go through before you get into town. They look at your driver's license and ask you where you're going and why. I don't think she would want to go through that gate because later she could be identified. "

"Good thinking Wilt," Dakota commented. "I'd rather see Bandelier. I read about the Pueblo people who lived in rock depression on high cliffs. They either carved out their homes or found carved out areas made by years of weather."

"True. It is very interesting to visit," Wilt said. "You can actually climb up into some of the caves that were used as houses. Maybe another time. Ahead is Santa Fe and on to Albuquerque. I'll talk to Frank Courts about what we found, or didn't find, while we were up at Jemez Springs."

* * *

Helcom sat in her SUV and kept watching the cars come and go in the apartment parking lot. She figured it was just a matter of time before Dakota arrived, parked her car, and started for her apartment. Helcom already knew what she was going to ask and how she would approach Dakota when she was headed for her living quarters. The shooting at Jemez area was already in the news and Helcom wanted to know what, if any, clues Dakota and Wilt may have gleamed from their trip to the crime scene. She knew she had to be careful and not ask too much and make Dakota suspicious.

After sitting for an hour and a half, Helcom began to wonder if she missed Dakota's arrival. About the time she was starting to exit Dakota drove in and parked near her apartment. Helcom immediately got out of her SUV and walked around the nearest corner to Dakota's door and waited.

As Dakota rounded the corner Helcom stepped out and walked toward her. "Well, hello," Helcom said. "Aren't you the lady who was at the shooting range the other day?"

Dakota, somewhat startled, took a moment before she answered. "Yes, I was there. Do you live here in this complex?

"Yes, I live in one-ten . I was just on my daily walk. I didn't know you also lived here. How nice it is to live near someone you know."

I'm not sure I like this person, Dakota thought. *She wasn't that friendly at the range.*

Helcom continued, "Maybe we can get together sometime to discuss our interests. Do you drink wine?"

Still a little guarded, Dakota responded, "Yes I drink wine, but I'm pretty busy with my job."

"I remember you said you were a police officer and were working to catch the sniper. I heard on the news that he struck again. Were you involved in that?"

"What do you mean involved?" answered Dakota.

"I mean were you asked to visit the site because the radio said the shooting was up around Jemez Springs."

"I really can't discuss an ongoing investigation." *I wish I had never said anything in the first place.*

"Oh, so you were there. At one time I wanted to be a police officer, or policewoman, but I was too heavy to make it through the training. Was it difficult?"

"I had just come out of the Army, so I was in shape and went right through," said Dakota.

"I don't want to keep you if you have something to do. It's just nice to talk to someone who knows what's going on. What did you do in the Army?"

"I really have to go. Maybe some other time I'll tell you about my Army experience, but I have some things to do right now," said Dakota as she started to walk around Helcom.

"OK, no problem. I'll catch you later. Maybe we can have breakfast sometime. Do you eat out or stay in? Helcom asked.

"I generally stop at Einstein Bros Bagels on Academy on my way to work." *Damn, why do I tell her these things!*

"I know the place. Maybe I'll see you there tomorrow morning."

Dakota turned and watched her go. *I don't know if she was just acting nice or pumping me for information. No, I think she was just surprised to see someone she knew and liked to talk. But in any case, I'll be on my toes around her.*

Helcom walked around the corner and headed for her car. *I didn't learn much, but I had to keep changing the subject so she would not suspect that I was looking for information. Perhaps next time I can get a little more. At lease I know where she goes for breakfast. I'll see if I can get some out of her tomorrow.*

Helcom went home and started to think about the next shooting.

* * *

Wilt phoned Frank Courts as soon as he reached his office. He could have called him any time before that but felt more comfortable talking in his office. He explained to Frank that there was really nothing to find at the shooting scene. They talked about the marks in the dirt around where the shooter was lying down. Wilt remarked about the bipod marks and how they could use that for confirming it was the same shooter as in Fort Sumner.

"The interesting thing," Wilt commented, "Is she now has moved out to sparsely populated areas. This is going to make it much more difficult to track her. The clues she is now giving are much broader than the first few."

"The bad news Wilt is that there is some talk about taking you off the job. We're paying you to get the shooter and so far no results. You need to step up your game or you will be out of a job," Frank said.

Wilt was silent for a moment. "Well, let's see what I have accomplished. First we now know the shooter is a woman, which is a major deal. Second, we know she traded her pickup in for an SUV in El Paso, and it was carrying Texas plates. Did the State Police stop any female driving a SUV with Texas plates recently? I'm sure she's stolen some New Mexico plates by now. Third, we know she's using a three-oh-eight caliber rifle, and we know what footprint the bipod leaves in the dirt. Forth we know her boot size from footprints we took from the shooting sights. We just need to solve one clue before she acts and we have her, with enough evidence to prove she is the serial shooter. That's not bad for a couple of weeks," Wilt said rather forcefully. "I would bet you would not have any of these things if it wasn't for Dakota and me being at the scene of the crimes and doing an outstanding job."

Frank responded, "You have some points Wilt. I'll make sure that the things you mention get back to those who are questioning your results."

"I appreciate that, Frank. If you want I can come in for a meeting and tell them myself, and if it's not good enough I can tell them to stick the information up their asses."

"Calm down Wilt. Just keep after the shooter and I'll handle the politics of this problem."

* * *

Helcom was thinking about her next shooting. She knew it was going to be difficult to continue hitting what she considered bad buys, but still wanted to be noticed. and wanted her next shooting to be close to something that was important to the community.

I wonder what I could do to the tram system. Everyone around here knows that the arial tramway goes from the bottom of the Sandia Mountain to the top, which is 6559 feet to 10,375 feet. Most people also know that the cable span between the second tower and the top of the mountain is the third longest span in the world. Plus, those tram cars carry up to fifty people at a time, with one going down and one coming up. What a target for a sniper to hide somewhere on the ground below the cars and shoot people as they go up and down. She got out her laptop and started looking at Google Earth. She had never climbed from the bottom of the tram system to the top of the mountain but thought she could see good shooting spots from looking at Google Earth. *There are a ton of places to hide as a shooter, but the big problem is planning an escape route. The police would have the mountain surrounded in no time and helicopters would be swirling overhead. There would be no way you would be able to get down or up the mountain without being seen. It would be a suicide mission. Probably should forget the tramway system as a target. I guess you could dig a hole and hide until all the people stopped looking, but that could be a couple of weeks. Nope, the cable system would be my last shooting so forget that.*

CHAPTER SEVENTEEN

The next morning Dakota stopped at the Einstein Bagel place and hesitated to get out of her car and enter the facility.

I kind of hate to go into get my breakfast because I don't want to run into the gal that lives in the complex that I met yesterday. But I'm hungry and she's not going to control my actions.

Taking a deep breath Dakota walked on in and looked around. She didn't see anyone she recognized, relaxed a little and ordered her favorite breakfast. She took an open table on the outside of the bagel house, sat down, looked up at the beautiful blue sky and puffy clouds and started eating her meal.

"Hello," said Helcom. Mind if I join you?'

"No, that would be fine," responded Dakota, *what choice do I have.*

"Good sandwiches and bagels," commented Helcom. "Think you could tell me what you did in the Army? I wanted to join the military, but I was told I'm too heavy. I'd like to lose weight, but it seems I just don't have the will power to stay away from food."

Maybe she's OK. Probably just lonely and looking for someone to talk to. "After a few jobs that I didn't like I was assigned to the Military Police, where I spent most of my time."

"So that's why you joined the Albuquerque Police?"

"Yes."

Helcom took a bite of her sandwich, chewed, and swallowed. "Are you into long range shooting? Is that why you want the steel targets? I thought police generally used a handgun for conflict."

Dakota thought for a moment, "They generally do. I was trained as a sniper in the Army."

"Really? I didn't know the military had female snipers."

"They don't but they let a few females go through the training, probably for political reasons."

"That's interesting." Helcom said as she continued to eat her sandwich. "What kind of rifle do you use?"

Dakota swallowed and said, "I have a Well Spec Ops MB134 with a scope and bipod."

"I shouldn't have asked that question because I don't even know what that is."

Dakota looked at Helcom and asked, "Do you shoot at the range?"

"I have a Thirty-Eight Special handgun and an old twenty-two single shot. I shoot those some of the time. The advantage of working out there is I get a discount when I use the range."

"You have a large family?" asked Dakota.

"Yes, I have four sisters. My father wanted a boy when I was born and didn't pay much attention to me as I was growing up." Helcom proceeded to talk about her family and her uncle and how her father ignored her.

After another fifteen minutes Dakota told Helcom she had to leave and get to work. She cleared their table and started for her car.

Dakota thought, *She's not so bad. I feel sorry for her based on how she grew up and how her father treated her. Maybe next time at the range I'll let her shoot my sniper rifle.* She got in her car and headed for the office.

Helcom continued to sit at her table and eat her sandwich and two bagels. Two men sat down at the next table and started talking. One told the other he was driving to Raton in two days to see a friend about a purchase of some stuff. He said he makes quite a bit of money selling the stuff to young people at the University of New Mexico.

Helcom listened carefully and found that the "stuff" was some kind of drugs. She deduced the talker would get to Raton around eleven thirty the day he was going because he said he was leaving at eight o'clock. She pretended to search for something in her purse but was looking at the individual who was the drug dealer. He was thin and had a full beard. She noticed the jewelry on his hands and the gold chain around his neck. He acted very self-assured, and she didn't like him even though she didn't know his name. She cleaned her table, walked to her car, and sat and waited for the two men to leave. She noticed the talker was driving a copper-colored Lexus SUV. She figured it would be easy to spot on Interstate 25 if she found the right location.

When she got home Helcom got out a map of New Mexico and started looking at various names of cities along Interstate 25. She kept looking until she came to a town called *Wagon Mound, now that's a strange name for a town.* She read about the history of the town. *This could be an interesting place for a freeway shoot. There are hills on either side of the small town and good places to be covered. Few people in the town. I'll drive up there tomorrow and check it out.* Helcom put the map away and walked into her kitchen to have an ice cream cup.

Helcom drove up to Wagon Mound the next day and did a reconnaissance of the area. *Perfect,* she thought. *On the south side of the road across from the Wagon Mound turn off you can see northbound cars coming a long way off. I can estimate the speed and take my shot just as the drug dealer gets to the turn off to the town. He'll be coming straight at me at a speed of probably around eighty miles an hour. That means he will probably go another quarter mile before his car runs off the road. In the confusion I can take the back road to Las Vegas, hit the Interstate 25 toward Albuquerque. Or I can take the long way around and end up in Tucumcari. If circumstances dictate I can always go north and stay in Raton, or Colorado Springs. I have many choices.* Smiling to herself, she started south toward Albuquerque.

* * *

Wilt was already in his office when Dakota walked in. He looked up at her and thought how attractive she was and said, "We need to get ourselves into a thinking mood and figure out where the shooter is going to hit next. I have been told that the people paying my salary want better results or I'm going to be canned."

"That's silly," exclaimed Dakota. "No one else could do any better."

"What have we missed during our investigation?"

Dakota thought for a minute. "Well, we have assumed all the targets are random. Maybe they are not. We know she took a couple of shots at you and one of those was not random."

"She had no idea that I would be at Billy the Kid's grave. That had to be random."

Dakota thought for a moment, "Perhaps the real target didn't show up and she picked you because you looked like you were interested more in her than looking at the grave."

"Maybe," mumbled Wilt. They both were silent for a minute. "I could go back and interview the families of the people she shot. Maybe something would come of that."

"At this point we have nothing else to do or to go on. Let's do that."

"I'll call Frank and let him know what we're going to do," Wilt said as he picked up his phone. When he connected with Frank Courts he explained his and Dakota's idea and it was approved immediately. "I'll need the names of those who were shot and shot at and missed," said Wilt.

"I can have that to you in the next hour," Frank said.

After the phone conversation ended, Wilt and Dakota talked about the targets. Wilt started the conversation. "If I remember, the first target was a guy driving east on Interstate forty. The shot missed and blew out his window. The second guy was shot going west and he was killed, plus there were some car wrecks involved in that one. The third victim was in Tucumcari, or coming back from somewhere and the shooter knew what time he'd be there."

Wilt's phone rang. Wilt pushed the phone image and Frank came on. "OK, here's the names. First, Fred Cooper who lives in Edgewood; George Holt, lives in Rio Rancho; William Rankin, lives in Rio Rancho; you, at Billy the Kids grave and you again at the Coronado Historical Site. The latest one is James Speed, who lives in Albuquerque. All of those named died from the shooter, except Fred Cooper and you, of course. I'll text the addresses to you. Please be gentle with the survivors. We talked to them all and could not find anything that connected them. All are white except William Rankin who is black. Strange that there were no Hispanic in the group, at least not yet. Good luck and keep me informed."

By the time the conversation with Frank ended, Dakota had the address of Fred Cooper in Edgewood. She hit her call button on her phone and waited for someone to answer. It went to a message machine, and it was a female voice that asked to leave a message. Dakota explained who she was and started to ask about Fred when the female voice interrupted her and explained they don't answer phone calls they don't recognize, but when she heard the word "detective" she answered. The woman explained that her husband was at work and gave Dakota his work number. After some more discussion Dakota clicked off and turned to Wilt.

"That was Fred's wife. She said they still have no idea who took a shot at Fred, but it has not happened again, so they decided it was a random shot. She gave me Fred's work number. Wilt called the number and asked the receptionist to ring Fred Cooper. Although he is a sales associate he was at his desk. Wilt explained who he was and wanted a few minutes of Fred's time regarding the shot at his car. An appointment was made in Fred's office in two hours.

Wilt and Dakota walked into the large equipment reception area and asked the receptionist for Fred Cooper. A few minutes later Fred walked up and introduced himself. Wilt and Dakota did the same thing and they walked back to Fred's small cubicle. Fred had to go and secure another chair for Dakota as there was only one extra chair in the cubicle.

Fred was a little less than six feet tall. He was wearing an open short sleeve plaid shirt and a pair of brown khakis. His office was organized with a few earthmoving models holding down small stacks of paper.

"So, you want to talk about who took a shot at me?" questioned Fred as he slid into his chair behind his desk. "Based on the fact that it has not happened again my wife and I decided it was a random event. You think it was connected to these other shootings around New Mexico?"

"We're not sure," explained Wilt. "It is something we are just now investigating. Do you know of anyone who would have wanted to shoot you?'

"I've been thinking about that for the last few days, and I can't think of anyone that I upset enough that they wanted to try and kill me."

Dakota asked, "What were your activities leading up to the shooting? What were you involved in a week or two prior to being shoot at?"

"I was just doing my job," said Fred. "I was involved in trying to sell a couple of earthmovers to a contractor for a job he had."

"Did you get the deal?" asked Wilt.

"Yeah, and boy was the Cat salesman pissed."

"Let me understand this." Said Wilt. "You got the deal, and you were competing against the Caterpillar salesman. I can understand why he might be a little upset, but was he mad enough to try and kill you?"

"I didn't think so. We compete all the time and he usually gets the deal because of what kind of guarantees Cat has. We bested him on this one. I was surprised when I heard he was upset so I called him and asked him if he shot at me."

"What was his response?" asked Dakota.

"He said if he wanted to kill me I would be dead already. He said he'd get the next deal. He said I was not worth going to jail over. I believed him and forgot about the situation."

Wilt asked for the competitive salesman's name and was told it was Manny Martinez. Dakota and Wilt thanked Fred and said goodbye. Once in the car they called and got an appointment with Manny and drove over to the Cat dealer. The same scenario played out again except the cubicle that Manny had was a little larger than Fred's.

Manny was a large man six feet four inches tall. He was big boned and had a protruding stomach. His voice went along with his size, and you could hear him talk through most of the sales office. He was dressed much like Fred Cooper with a short sleeve shirt and slacks.

"Did you tell many people that you had lost the sale to Fred Cooper?" asked Wilt.

"Yeah, I told a bunch of people, especially my boss. Fred represents low quality equipment but came through with a program that we couldn't match, so the sale went to him. Now I'm going to have to fight his program every time I come up against him."

"So, you have no idea who took a shot at Fred Cooper?" asked Dakota.

"Sorry I can't help you there. Generally, the salesmen I know don't try and kill their competition each time they lose a deal. Wouldn't be many salesmen left if that were the case."

"What do you do for relaxing?" asked Dakota.

"I should read salesmen's books," said Manny half joking. "Sometimes I go to the Albuquerque shooting range and empty a box of shells with my nine-millimeter."

Wilt and Dakota walked out and got back into the car. "Maybe we're chasing out tails on this," said Wilt.

"Who knows where this will lead us. We need to at least try a couple more before we give up on this idea," explained Dakota.

The next individual was shot going west on Interstate forty in a red pickup. His name was George Holt and had a small business washing industrial machinery. He was killed when the shooter shot him through the windshield. His home was located in a nice part of Rio Rancho. Dakota had called ahead and talked to George's wife and after some conversation his wife relented and agreed to see her and Wilt.

Mrs. Holt was a well coiffured woman who was a little on the plump side. She wore a bouse and slacks. She welcomed Wilt and Dakota into her house and offered something to drink, which both declined. After some small conversation and offers of condolences, Wilt began the conversation.

"Mrs. Holt do you have any idea why your husband was targeted by the shooter while he was going toward Grants?"

"I've thought long and hard about his murder and I keep coming up with more questions than answers. Do we know if he was a target or was it a random shooting and he was just in the wrong place at the wrong time?"

"That's what we are trying to determine. If he was targeted and we found why, it might lead us to the killer," said Dakota.

"I wish I could do more, but I can't."

"We would like to talk to some of the people at your husband's office. Who should we contact for permission to hold interviews?" asked Wilt.

Mrs. Holt's mood changed, and her face became flushed, "I'm the president of the company right now. We don't have a secretary because I fired her. I never approved of her low-cut blouses and short skirts. I suspected my husband was having an affair with that little filly, but he always denied it. Anyway, she's gone. You can contact Henry Gonzales as I put him in charge. Tell him we talked, and I approved you two going down there and talking about George. I'll get you the address and phone number."

A little while later, Wilt and Dakota were at the office of the former George Holt. It was a small company with ten people in the office and some service trucks and other personnel cars parked outside. Henry Gonzales was a pleasant man but didn't have much information about why George Hole was shot.

"In the last year George spent most of his time chasing Lilly, our former secretary."

"Do you think that got him in trouble?" asked Dakota.

"I don't see how, unless Stella, his wife, put out a hit on him," said Henry. "That's highly unlikely. The secretary wasn't married so I don't think there was any pissed off boyfriend involved. In any case she didn't mention one."

"Did George have any habits, other that the secretary?" asked Wilt.

"He played golf once in a while. About every month we'd go to the shooting range. He liked to take his shotgun out and shoot trap. That's about it."

"We appreciate your time Henry. If you can think of anything else that might help us please let us know," and Wilt handed him his calling card.

Afterward in the car both Wilt and Dakota were silent as they were occupied with their own thoughts.

"I don't know how productive it will be, but let's go talk to William Rankin's wife to see if we can get anything from her about William being a target."

"What's the difference between Trap and Skeet?" asked Dakota.

"They are both shotgun shooting sports. Trap throws clay birds out in front of you in various directions going away from you, simulating a bird taking off from the ground. Skeet throws the clay disks across higher in front of you simulating bird, or ducks, in flight. Both have different shooting stations that you move after a certain number of shots."

"Which one is more difficult?" asked Dakota.

"I have found that I can generally hold my own with Trap. I can usually get upwards of twenty hits out of twenty-five tries. Skeet is another story. I call them super birds because by the time I get my shotgun aimed and ready to fire the clay birds are already gone. I can get the ones going away from me or coming directly at me, but the ones going across are not my cup of tea."

They again were silent as they looked for the Rankin's house. They found it on the corner of the street. It was a two-story house with a few trees and a rock yard. It was nicely painted and had a small front porch. At first Mrs. Rankin was hesitant to let them come inside but once Dakota showed her the police badge she relented, and they went inside. The house was small but well decorated and tidy. There was a keyboard in one corner, which Wilt was going to use as an ice breaker.

"Mrs. Rankin we are very sorry about your loss," Wilt began, "And we are here to see if you know any reason why someone would want to shoot your husband?"

"No," replied Mrs. Rankin. "William was a diligent worker and did quite well."

"I see a keyboard in the corner, did he play?"

Mrs. Rankin looked at the keyboard and said, "Yes. He would put earphones on and play for an hour or two when he was upset about something."

Dakota asked, "What was he generally upset about?"

Mrs. Rankin hesitated, "Every time he thought about the government controls and their interference into his work, he got upset. He even refused to pay his taxes for a couple of years, but finally relented."

"Did he play golf or go to the shooting range?" asked Wilt.

"No. His release was that keyboard," was Mrs. Rankin's answer.

"What kind of business was he in?" asked Dakota.

"He worked at the Sandia Lab," his wife said. "Even though we talked several time about what he did I'm not sure I ever understood his work. Something about parts for nuclear weapons."

"Yes, it's pretty secret over there," Wilt said.

After they left both Wilt and Dakota didn't talk at first, keeping their thoughts to themselves.

Dakota broke the silence and said, "Why did you ask Mrs. Rankin if her husband played golf or spent time at the shooting range?"

"Well, it's the only thing the I could think of. Manny Gonzales and George Holt both went to the shooting range, but Fred Cooper didn't. Only George Holt played golf. I was just trying to get some commonality in the victims. Didn't get much."

"Even if you didn't get much it's a good idea. By-the-way do you know what they do at the Sandia Lab?"

Wilt thought for a moment. "Their primary mission is to **develop, engineer, and test the non-nuclear components of nuclear weapons and high technology.**"

"**Oh, that tells me a lot. Thanks, now I really understand their mission,**" **said Dakota with sarcasm in her voice.**

"**Sandia came into existence in nineteen forty-five. The Manhattan project needed an offsite testing area for non-nuclear components. They set up a lab outside of Los Alamos and it became Sandia National Laboratories. Today it's** head-quartered on Kirtland Air Force Base in Albuquerque, it also has a campus in Livermore, California, next to Lawrence Livermore," added Wilt.

"That's enough," said Dakota. "I got the idea of what they do, kind-of."

Wilt's cell phone rang. He looked at the name of the caller, "It's Frank Courts, I better take it. Hello Frank."

"Anything from your interviews?" asked Frank.

"Nothing we can use. We can't find anything in common with the people who she shot at."

"Well, we have another clue," said Frank.

"Let me put my phone on speaker. OK, Dakota is with me so she can hear it also."

"The clue is: *They could see it for miles on the Santa Fe Trail.* That's it. We figure it has to be somewhere between Raton and Santa Fe along Interstate twenty-five."

"Thanks," said Wilt. "Dakota and I will see what we can come up with. Anything else?"

"Nope. Keep working on this case, Wilt. We appreciate what you and Dakota have come up with and looking forward to more."

Wilt clicked off. He looked at Dakota and said, "Well, that's some clue. It has to be along I-twenty-five like Frank said."

"Why?' asked Dakota. "Is that where the Santa Fe Trail goes?"

"Yes, it originally came out of Franklin, Missouri but later moved to Independence, Missouri. It went from Missouri through Kansas, Oklahoma, Colorado and ended up in Santa Fe. It came over Raton Pass in New Mexico and stayed pretty close to where the I-twenty-five is today. There are a couple of variations but that was the main route. It was roughly nine hundred miles long."

"What was its main purpose?" she asked.

"It was primarily a commerce route, but the Apache and Comanche didn't think so and gave many travelers grief as they came west. There is a lot of information about the Santa Fe trail on the Internet, and it's been written about countless times in Western books. It was the main route before the railroad replaced it."

"Did a lot of people use the trail before the trains came?" asked Dakota.

"I read once that it was hard to tell because of the record keeping. One statistic showed that between eighteen forty-nine and eighteen fifty-nine twelve thousand people traveled the Santa Fe Trail, along with three thousand wagons and fifty thousand animals."

"Wow, that's a bunch of people. When did the trains get to Raton?"

"The trains came in eighteen eighty. After that the Santa Fe Trail faded into history."

"What do you think about the current clue?" asked Dakota.

"There are a few things that can be seen for miles on the Trail. The Raton Pass is one of them. Wagon Mound is another. Let's look at your laptop and see what comes up?"

Dakota opened her laptop, went to Google, and typed in "Things you can see from the Santa Fe Tail in New Mexico."

"Four things have come up," said Dakota. "They are Rabbit Ears Mountain; Starvation Peak; Raton Pass; and Wagon Mound."

"What do they say about the first two?" asked Wilt.

"Rabbit Ears Mountain. The double peak of Rabbit Ears Mountain directed travelers on the Cimarron Route of the Santa Fe Trail toward their destination. Visible across the prairies in present-day Oklahoma and Eastern New Mexico, the mountain was a vital landmark for guiding weary, disoriented travelers and a sign that restorative water, and grazing grass was ahead.

"Starvation peak is a butte that sits at over seven thousand feet, located along Interstate twenty-five between the town of Pecos and Las Vegas. A prominent landmark to motorists on the highway today, it was also a noted landmark on the Santa Fe Trail."

"The Cimarron Route came later and didn't really follow the Interstate twenty-five. Let's look at the Raton Pass and Wagon Mound. What do they say about them?" asked Wilt.

"The Raton Pass was treacherous, and many wagons, animals and men were lost trying to get from Colorado to New Mexico. You could see the pass from a long ways on the Trail."

Dakota continued, "Wagon Mound has a mountain that looks like one of the covered wagons, the Conestoga Wagon. Today it is along the I-twenty-five and the mound on the hill can be seen for one hundred and twenty-five miles from the top of Raton Pass."

Wilt thought for a moment before he spoke, "I think that's where our shooter is going to make the next hit. You can see cars coming north for quite a distance and since hardly anyone knows about Wagon Mound it would be a nice area to take a shot. It is a National Historic Landmark so it would get a lot of press. Plus, there are several back roads you can take to get back to Albuquerque."

"When do you think she'll strike?" asked Dakota.

"I'd guess in the next day or two. We should probably head up that direction and start covering the area. Maybe we can get the jump on her before she sets up."

"Is there a place to stay in Wagon Mound?"

Wilt thought a moment, "Not really. We'll stay in Las Vegas in the Plaza Hotel. It will be a real treat and the price is very competitive. It's forty miles south from Wagon Mound but we can get there early and stay late each day. I had better let Frank Courts know what we are planning to do. If they think the clue is the same as we do we may have a crowd up there."

Wilt put in a call to Courts. The consensus of opinion of the police was the answer centered around the Raton Pass. Wilt explained his reasoning behind his choice of Wagon Mound but didn't press the idea because he didn't want anyone to come to where they were going to be.

"OK, you and Dakota take Wagon Mound and we'll have people stationed in various places along Raton Pass. Good luck."

It didn't take long for Wilt and Dakota to make reservations at the Plaza, grab their "go bags" and head out for Las Vegas, New Mexico.

CHAPTER EIGHTEEN

Helcom got out of bed early that morning. She knew she wanted to be in place for the shoot early in the morning because she didn't want to miss her target. She left for Wagon Mound at four in the morning. She figured none of the four hundred and sixty-two people who lived there would be up moving around at six in the morning. She needed time to set up her equipment without being seen.

When she arrived at her destination the first thing to do was to find a place to park the car. Helcom chose a small spot behind a few trees that were not far off the road. It took her three trips up the small hill along the road to find the shooting spot. There was no problem seeing vehicles coming a quarter mile away. She got in a relaxed position, started looking through her binoculars and waited.

She was still waiting for the copper-colored Lexus SUV when she saw Dakota and Wilt arrive. They pulled into one of the two filling stations that were along the interstate and got out of their car.

Shit, she thought. *I guess my clue was too easy. Now I decide to go ahead and hit the target and try to get out of here, or just let him pass and try again later.* She sat there thinking. *Maybe I could do both. I could hit my target, turn, and drop either Wilt or Dakota, which would delay them from trying to catch me as they would be consumed with the wounded or dead partner. Putting a bullet in a tire would delay them further. What the hell, you only live once and I'm here and see them and they don't know where I am.*

Helcom kept her eyes on Wilt and Dakota and also on the road where the copper-colored Lexus would be coming from. She noticed Wilt and Dakota were in a close huddle discussing something.

They are trying to figure out where I am and how to find me. She noticed when they broke the huddle both crossed the road to her side. Dakota was starting to climb the hill in front of her and it looked like Wilt would search the hill behind her. She estimated Dakota was one hundred yards in front of her. Just as Dakota disappeared behind some heavy brush, Helcom saw her target coming up the road. She put her scope on the car's windshield, estimated the distance and speed of the car, placed the crosshairs on the middle of the hood and pulled the trigger. She immediately took her head away from the rifle scope and chambered another round, looking to see if she could spot Dakota out in front of her. She heard the tires screech and the noise of the Lexus as it went off the side of the road and started rolling over. Dakota came into view and Helcom quickly put the crosshairs on her left chest and shot again. Dakota jerked backward and went out of sight. Helcom quickly put another round in the chamber and took aim at the car parked at the filling station and put a round in the front right tire. She figured Wilt was coming up somewhere behind her and hollered out "The woman has been shot," thinking that would redirect Wilt's search. She got on her knees and looked behind her and spotted Wilt just as he was running down the hill back to the road.

Helcom grabbed her gear and moved as quickly as she could down the hill toward her car. She threw the gear in the back and jumped in the front seat. Starting the car she headed north, figuring the police would think she would go south toward Albuquerque. Her plan was to head north to Springer, take the road to Cimarron and stay in the St. James Hotel tonight. She could take the back road to Las Vegas tomorrow or the next day and on to Albuquerque when it was clear. She noticed the copper-colored Lexus was upside down off the side of the road in the middle of a cloud of dust. Helcom surmised she had hit her primary target.

*** * ****

Wilt and Dakota also left early that morning for Wagon Mound. They both knew that their supposition that the shooter would be in that area could be wrong. Wilt didn't say anything, but he knew if he was wrong he may lose his financial relationship with the Albuquerque Police Department. That would be bad enough, but he didn't want to lose being with Dakota every day.

I guess I'm to the point that I really like her. He thought. *I'm getting used to her company and look forward to seeing her every day.,* He looked over at her while he was driving.

She caught his stare and said, "What?"

"Oh nothing," responded Wilt. "I was just worried about you getting hurt when we start our search for the shooter."

"What if she's not there and we are wrong? She could be over in Raton Pass, or someplace else altogether."

"We'll cross that bridge when we come to it. I just wanted to say how much I have enjoyed having you as a partner. I look forward to seeing you each day, and you always have good advice and ideas,."

"Thank you," said Dakota with her face a little flushed. "I enjoy you too Wilt, a lot."

They both rode in silence for a few minutes.

"Any chance I could go into partnership with you when this whole thing is over?" Asked Dakota. "I've been thinking about it, and I think we make a good pair, and the Morrison/Chavez Agency has a nice ring to it. With my last name we could probably pull in more Hispanics than before."

Wilt was a little surprised she was thinking that direction. "I don't know," he said. He quickly followed, "I like the idea, Dakota. We'd have to pencil it out to see what it would take financially to survive. Yes, the more I think about it, the more I like it."

"What are the requirements to get a private eye license in New Mexico?" she asked.

"You have to be at least eighteen years old and be a resident of the United States. You can't have any felony, domestic violence, or abuse convictions, and have no convictions involving the illegal use or possession of a deadly weapon or violent act. You must have a high school diploma and have completed at least six thousand hours of investigative experience within the past five years, along with mandatory firearms training. Last but not least is a written exam," recited Wilt from memory.

"Six thousand hours? That's a hell of a lot of needed hours," exclaimed Dakota.

"I got a waver because of my military and detective training," said Wilt. "Maybe you could get some of those hours reduced because of your military and police training."

Dakota started to say something else when Wilt interrupted her, "There's Wagon Mound. You can see how it looks like a wagon. We need to think how we're going to approach the shooter. We'll park and take a look at the terrain and decide from there."

Wilt parked the car in a gas station parking area where they had a good view across the interstate where the shooter might be. They exited the car and stood looking at the hills.

"It looks to me like she may be after a car coming south from Raton because you can see further looking north from the hill than you can south," Wilt said.

"If she has reasons to pick a particular target that means he or she is coming from the Albuquerque direction," said Dakota.

"I agree, but we don't know that yet."

"What about our weapons? Are we going to take them up the hill with us or set them up from here?" Dakota asked.

Wilt thought for a moment, "I think once she shoots her target she will want to get out of here as quickly as possible so she will be carrying her gear and running for the car. All we need to do is watch where she goes and try and get back to our car and intercept her before she leaves. In any case we'll know what she's driving and what direction she's going."

"I don't know, Wilt," said Dakota as she looked toward the hill. "She obviously knows we're here now if she's paying attention to what's going on around her. She may be packing up and leaving as we're standing here."

"You're right. You take the left part of the hill and I'll take the right. Let's see if we can spot her as she leaves."

As Wilt started to move, he thought. *I'm sure she will be shooting toward Raton Pass so I'll take that direction which will be in her line of site if she's still on the hill. Dakota will be coming up behind her and be safer.*

A few steps into the hill, Wilt heard a shot. He ducked because he couldn't tell from which direction the shot was aimed. He looked up as he heard some car tires screech and the sound of metal scraping against hard packed earth. He heard the second shot.

What the hell, she's not shooting again at the car. DAKOTA! Shit, Shit, Shit,

Wilt heard a third shot and the sound of a bullet hitting steel or iron. He heard the shooter yell, "The woman has been shot." Without hesitation he turned around and started running back toward the interstate, thinking all the time of Dakota.

Wilt continued to run along the interstate. He noticed the car which had been the target had rolled over several times as it came to rest along the side of the road. Several people were running toward it apparently to figure out the condition of the driver. Wilt reached the area where Dakota had started up the hill.

"Dakota!" he yelled as he climbed the hill. He kept yelling her name as he ran in between the brush. Halfway up the hill he saw her, lying on her back in the dirt. There was blood underneath her shoulder and her eyes were closed. She was not moving.

"Dakota," Wilt said as he reached her. She opened her eyes and closed them again without saying anything. "Wilt put his handkerchief under her shoulder, and she groaned with pain. He took out his phone and pushed 911. The operator came on and Wilt explained the situation and the magic phrase was "Officer Down." He requested a medical helicopter to land at Wagon Mound and take Dakota to the hospital in Albuquerque. He guessed that the bullet had hit her just under the collar bone and gone clear through because of the blood on her back. He yelled for someone to help get her down to the area where a helicopter could land. One resident handed him blankets which he wrapped her in. Another resident gave him two sterile gauze pads which he presses on both sides of her body where she had been shot.

Wilt kept talking to her trying to get her to open her eyes, which she did off and on for a few seconds. He talked and rocked her body trying to keep her awake. It seemed like an eternity before he heard the sound of the helicopter coming, but it was actually forty-five minutes. The paramedics jumped out of the chopper when it landed and took control of Dakota and put her on a gurney and into the helicopter. One of the paramedics started an I.V. as the copper lifted off the ground and started back. Wilt felt the dust in from the whirling blades in his hair, but it didn't matter. All he could think about was Dakota. He realized he had an empty feeling inside. As he watched the helicopter disappear he understood just how much he cared for her.

Dear God please let her live and recover, he thought as his eyes welled up with tears, *I have to get to the hospital in Albuquerque.*

As he walked back to his car, he remembered the third shot and knew the shooter had punctured one of his tires. He prepared himself to discover the flat tire and hoped the bullet did not do any damage to the wheel or it would be a long time before he got to Albuquerque. Much to his amazement he saw three men around his car as they pulled off the ruined tire and had a spare ready to install.

"We figured you'd be in a hurry to get back to the big city, so we thought we'd help you along. We popped your trunk and got your spare," said one of the men.

"I just checked your wheel, and it looks OK," said another man.

"I really don't know what to say," mumbled Wilt. "Can I pay you something."

"No, we just wanted to help."

As Wilt was getting in the car he asked, "Did anyone check on the guy driving the wrecked car?"

"Yes, we went over to see if he was alright. It looks like a bullet got him in the forehead and the car is a total mess. We'll let the police figure it all out."

Wilt asked, "Did anyone see which way the shooter went?"

"He went north," replied one. "He may be heading for Raton, or somewhere in Colorado."

Wilt heard sirens coming from the north. "The police will be here in a moment. If they ask about me tell them I'm heading for the University hospital in Albuquerque. I'll check in with them and they can find me there." He turned on the car, drove to the interstate and floored the accelerator.

It's a hundred and sixty-five miles to Albuquerque, interstate all the way. I've got a half tank of gas and its light traffic, I'll make it in two hours, or die trying!

His phone rang as he was going through Las Vegas. It was Frank Courts. "What the hell happened?" Courts yelled.

"I miscalculated," said Wilt. "I was sure that the shooter was going for someone coming from the north, not the south. I didn't think we were in time to stop her, but I wanted to find which direction she chose for her escape route. If we knew that, we'd have a good chance of catching her because of the limited routes away from Wagon Mound. I sent Dakota to cover the south and I went to cover the north thinking I had the dangerous direction. I was wrong. The shooter got her target and figured if she shot one of us the other would be pre-occupied and she'd escape. She shot Dakota, and after that the tire on my car. I was so busy with trying to save Dakota that I didn't see where the shooter went. Onlookers told me she went north toward Raton. I'm on my way to the hospital in Albuquerque and just went past Las Vegas."

"How's Dakota?" asked Courts.

"Looks like she was shot just under the left clavicle. Not necessarily a fatal wound if the bullet went all the way through, but she lost a lot of blood while we were waiting for a medivac."

"You sure the bullet didn't hit a major artery?"

"Frank, right now I'm not sure about anything except worrying about Dakota."

"OK, see you at the hospital. Bye."

Wilt continued to drive south on I-25 until he reached the University Hospital. He pulled in a spot, jumped out of the car, and rushed into the main reception area. It took about five minutes for the desk people to locate Dakota because she was in surgery. Wilt went up to the surgery waiting room and saw that Frank Courts was already there, along with Georgie.

"Has anyone any news?" asked Wilt as he looked at Georgie with a surprised look on his face.

"All we know now is she has lost a lot of blood, but the doctor thinks she has a chance because she's young and strong," responded Frank.

"I know you are surprised to see me, Wilt. Frank called me and told me what happened and thought you might need some company through this. I hope you don't mind," said Georgie.

Wilt looked at Georgie and noticed how pretty she looked. "No, I don't mind. Thanks for coming over Georgie."

* * *

Helcom loaded her equipment in her SUV and wasted no time getting back on the I-25 going north toward Raton. She was confident that most of the individuals that were awake and at the two filling stations in Wagon Mound would be preoccupied with the overturned car that was resting in the dust alongside the road just north of the two stations. She proceeded north glancing at her rear-view mirror every ten seconds. She did pass one state patrol car going south with their lights blinking and siren on. She didn't think the person driving the patrol car saw her since the interstate was four lanes, each two lanes separated by a wide median. She drove for 20 minutes to Springer, New Mexico and turned left on to State Highway 58 towards Cimarron. In another 25 minutes she pulled up to the St James hotel in Cimarron and checked into the room that she called ahead and booked when she was on her way from Wagon Mound. After getting organized she took a nap, and in the early evening ate a nice dinner in the St James dining room. Back in her hotel room she began thinking, *I should take it easy for a while. That situation in Wagon Mound was too close to getting caught. I hated to shoot Dakota, but I really had no choice. Too bad Wilt didn't come up in front of me and I could have dropped him. I hope Dakota is OK as I took a quick aim just above her heart. When I get back to Albuquerque it should be old news so I could visit her in the hospital, if she made it through. I'm sure it's in the papers because not much happens in Wagon Mound and if someone got shot there ought to be big news, plus the car wreck and the officer getting wounded. I suspect they will be looking for me in the Raton area, and probably even in Colorado.*

Helcom spent a restless night in the Jessie James room and because the hotel offered no breakfast she had breakfast at the Cimarron Mercantile across the street. She filled the car with fuel and keeping to the back roads she took the two-hour trip to Taos on state highway sixty-four. It was a beautiful ride through the mountains along the Cimarron River. When she arrived at Taos she turned on to highway 518 toward Las Vegas, which was another two and a half hours. She stayed on highway 518 until she arrived at Mora. She thought about turning right on highway 68 because it was not used much but she didn't like the looks of it, so she stayed on the 518. When she arrived in Las Vegas she once again put fuel in her vehicle and drove to the Plaza Hotel and checked in. She bought a paper and read about the shooting in Wagon Mound. The paper mentioned the man who was killed and also the police officer who was wounded. The paper went on to say the officer was in critical condition and there was an all-points bulletin out for the killer. The police chief of the state patrol stated that this was the fifth person the shooter had killed, plus three misses. The chief went on to say that the shooter was considered a Serial Killer and would be brought to justice quickly.

Helcom had dinner at Charlie's Spic & Span Restaurant and went to bed early. She had trouble going to sleep and started thinking about her next shot. *Rather than shooting someone who I think deserves it maybe my target should be in a famous or historical place. That seems to get more attention.*

Ideas when through her head about famous places in New Mexico.

She settled on the Ghost Ranch in Abiquiu, Northern New Mexico.

Everyone knows about Georgia O'Keeffe, the famous New Mexico painter. If I shot someone on her ranch, it would be big news.

Helcom when to sleep with a smile on her face thinking about how she would set up her target and get a killing in that well known place.

CHAPTER NINETEEN

"How long has she been in surgery?" asked Wilt.

"A couple of hours. They took her in right after they got here," said Frank.

Wilt walked over to a row of chairs and sat down. Georgie walked over and sat down beside him. She reached over and took his hand. They both sat there and said nothing.

"I got a call from the chief," said Frank. "He wanted to know what happened and how Dakota was. I had a long conversation about you, which we will discuss."

"I figured that," said Wilt as he took a deep breath and let it out.

"My basic question is why you sent her up the hill on the south side, the same direction the shooter was aiming."

"We'll talk about it after we find out how the surgery comes out," said Wilt. "Right now, I'd like to sit here and pray for Dakota."

"I'm sure she will be fine," said Georgie, squeezing Wilt's hand.

Wilt looked at Georgie. She had on a white blouse and blue pants and high heels. The blouse was cut low in front showing some of her cleavage. The pants were cut tight, and the high heels accentuated her slim figure.

Damn, Georgie looks good. What is wrong with me?

The doctor walked in the room and went straight to Frank. "The surgery went very well and she's still in critical condition, but things look good. We repaired her shoulder, and she should make a full recovery. She'll be in a shoulder cast for a few weeks and will need some rehab, but she's strong and will do well."

"Thank God," said Wilt.

"Will she be able to go back to full duty?" Frank asked.

"No doubt about it," said the doctor. "The only thing that was damaged was soft tissue, but that takes a while to heal. Any other questions?"

Frank looked at Wilt and Georgie and both shook their heads.

"Thank you doctor," Frank said. "When can we see her?"

"I'd suggest you wait until tomorrow. It's going to take a while for her to come out of the aesthetic and we'll keep her sedated for the pain. I'd suggest tomorrow would be best."

"Has anyone notified her parents?" asked Georgie.

"I'm going back to the office and look in her file and get their contact information. I wanted to know how she was before I called them," responded Frank. "I have to talk to Wilt," said Frank. "Can you wait downstairs Georgie?"

"That's not a problem for me, I'll wait," said Georgie rolling her eyes when Frank could not see her face. "I think you need some company for a while. I'll fix dinner and make sure you make it home," said Georgie. She went downstairs and sat down.

"I'm not pleased when one of my people gets shot Wilt, what the fuck happened up there?" said Frank.

"I tried to protect her, but I screwed up," said Wilt as he looked at Frank right in the eyes. "I figured the shooter's target was coming from the north, but it was coming from the south. I sent Dakota in the wrong direction."

"Why did you climb the hill at all"? asked Frank.

"I wanted to find the shooter before she shot her target. If I was too late and she had already taken the shot she would be moving back to her car where I would intercept and take her down. If I was later than that at lease I'd see her car and know which direction she was taking for her escape route."

"The big screw up was guessing the target was coming from the wrong direction," said Frank. "Why did you think he was coming from the north?"

"If you look at the terrain you'll see that the road leading from the north is straighter for a longer distance coming into Wagon Mound. The shooter would have more time to calculate the details for the shot. I thought that was a better choice than trying to hit a target coming from the south."

"So, you sent Dakota into the sights of the shooter," said Frank. "How else did you screw this up?"

"I should have known that the shooter would see us arrive and know we were there. She had time to figure out an escape plan. When she saw Dakota coming up the hill she figured if she shot her I would be too busy trying to save Dakota that I would not try to block her exit. She was right."

"So, you're saying her target came just in time for her to shoot him, then to shoot Dakota, and to shoot the car." asked Frank. "If she knew you were behind her why didn't she turn around and shoot you rather than Dakota?"

"I asked myself the same question. The shooter was in a time pinch. She had to shoot one of us in order to stop us from finding her. Dakota was in the same line of sight that her target was, so it was faster to shoot Dakota than turn around, find me, resight her rifle and fire. Besides as soon as I heard the shot I hit the deck."

"How did you know Dakota was shot?" questioned Frank.

"After the third shot the shooter yelled at me and said that the woman was shot. At once I started down the hill and headed over to find Dakota."

Frank asked, "How did the shooter know you have feelings for Dakota? You think she knows you?"

Wilt thought for a moment. "I believe the shooter knew that any partnership of law enforcement has a strong bond between them, and one would do most anything to save their partner. One can find this strength of partnership from watching police shows on the Internet. I don't think the shooter knows me." He hesitated, "It wouldn't be hard to find who I am because of the internet and my web page."

Frank's phone rang. Frank put the phone to his ear and said, "Did they find the shooter?" After a few minutes Frank said, "I'm talking to him right now. I'll let him know," and clicked off. Frank stood there looking at Wilt without saying anything. He took a deep breath, let it out and said, "The highway patrol reported they still have not found the shooter. I have been given the order of suspending our relationship with you and taking you license and weapon until a thorough investigation is completed."

Wilt felt his temper rising and his face getting red. "What the hell, I didn't shoot her."

"I know but it certainly can be considered poor judgement," responded Frank.

"All my decisions can be explained and were logical, including holding compressions on her wounds until the helicopter came. That probably saved her life."

Frank said, "We have a serial killer on the loose and limited resources. So far you are the only one that has figured out where and when the shooter was going to be from the clues. We have missed every location and would be further behind than we are now. I have to do something to satisfy my boss, so I'm taking you off the case. You can keep your license and weapon, but you are no longer going to be given information about the shooter, or any clues that may come in. I don't want to see you at any meeting about the shooter or show up at any crime scene. Do you understand?"

At first Wilt didn't say anything. "Speaking of an error in judgement Frank, you just made a major mistake. I think we are close to getting this person, but this will put you back almost to square one." He turned around and walked down the stairs.

* * *

On the way to Georgie's house Wilt was pensive. He told Georgie about his conversation with Frank and how pissed off he got. She thought, based on the circumstances, that Frank probably did the least he could do and still satisfy the department and other law enforcement elements. She asked Wilt what he was going to do, and he told her he was going to continue to work to stop the shooter because he felt he owed it to Dakota.

They didn't talk much on the rest of the way to Georgie's house. Once inside Georgie asked Wilt to get them both a glass of wine while she washed her face and hands. Wilt secured the wine, poured two glasses, sat down in the family room, and waited. Georgie returned, sat across from Wilt, and took a sip of her wine.

"Are you in love with Dakota?" she asked.

The question surprised Wilt. He thought a moment, "I don't know. I like being around her and she does a good job and makes a good partner, but I don't know if my feelings run that deep."

"How did you feel when you learned she was shot?"

"I felt scared, worried, and mad all at the same time, "replied Wilt.

"What were your feelings this afternoon when you saw me?" Georgie asked.

"That's a good question, Georgie. I thought you looked attractive and sexy. I questioned myself as to why I didn't love you."

"You know that I still have very strong feelings about you. I still say I'm in love with you. When Frank called I jumped at the opportunity to see you again even though the circumstances were not the best. I can offer you a lot, Wilt."

"Georgie…"

"Let me finish," she interrupted. "My strong feelings for you would be the cornerstone of our marriage. I would make you a good wife. You wouldn't need to worry when your business is slow because I have the means to support you in bad times. I would show you some of the best things in New Mexico. We would have season tickets to Broadway shows and symphony concerts and we'd go to the best restaurants. I'd like to introduce you to the powerful people in Santa Fe. There is nothing I wouldn't do for you Wilt. I would strive to make you happy and work to help you with your business. Plus, I'm sure we would have a great sex life."

Wilt just sat there. He didn't know what to say. "I don't know what causes people to be attracted to one another. I think it's a combination of responses, mostly which cannot be controlled by the individual. I like you Georgie. I like being around you and I like our sex, but I don't have an empty feeling when I'm not with you. I don't feel an urge to be with you again. I don't know why, it's just not there."

"I have our dinner in the oven. It's time to take it out, so let's go into the dining room and continue our conversation if it's necessary," she said.

Once again Wilt felt some muscle tension as he walked into the dining room. He didn't know why he always felt a wave of guilt when he told Georgie his true feelings.

During dinner, the conversation turned to what Wilt and Dakota had been doing in their quest to catch the shooter. Wilt also talked about educating Dakota about the various towns and elements of New Mexico.

The dinner was an excellent spicy meatloaf that Georgie had put together. The sides were corn and peas.

"I have some ice cream cups for dessert, topped off with black berries and blueberries.

"The meatloaf was delicious," commented Wilt. "The wine was a nice choice and went very well with the meal."

"Thanks. I chose a Beaujolais Village because I like a nice light French red wine."

"Do you always put a slight chill on the reds?" asked Wilt as he noticed his wine was not room temperature.

"I have found I enjoy a red wine slightly chilled. I keep my red wine cooler at sixty degrees Fahrenheit. It's a little too cool if you drink it when it comes right out of the cooler but warms up a little when you let it breath."

"Interesting. I enjoyed it a little cooled," said Wilt.

"Will you spend the night with me Wilt?" asked Georgie.

Wow that question came out of nowhere, thought Wilt. Several images flashed through his mind. One was Georgie's naked body and her smooth skin. Another was holding her and climaxing together. *What the hell should I do? I really would like to stay but it would just make leaving more difficult. I don't want to hurt her feelings, so maybe just this time. I could use some stress release. What the hell you only live once. But there's Dakota.*

"I think that would be really nice but with all that has happened today I'm just worn out. I think it best you take me back to my car and we call it a night."

Georgie sat there looking at Wilt, "Want some dessert?"

"The dinner and wine were excellent, Georgie. I'm not used to eating this much and I'm really full. I think I'll pass on dessert."

"OK. Let's get you home."

Georgie got up from the table and Wilt did the same. He picked up his plate and started to put the silverware on it to carry it to the kitchen.

"Leave it on the table Wilt. I'll clean things up when I return. I have nothing else to do this evening."

Wilt felt a wave of guilt flow over him again and placed the plate back on the table. He followed Georgie out to her car and climbed in. Neither one of them spoke until they were in the hospital parking lot next to Wilt's car.

"I really appreciate your company tonight," said Wilt. It was so much better than me being alone. It was also nice seeing you again Georgie and thanks for dinner."

"Take care of yourself," she said with moisture in her eyes. "I hope to see you again sometime."

"I'm sure you will." He exited the car and got into his SUV. As he backed out of his parking place he watched Georgie leave the parking lot. *She really is a nice lady* he thought. *Maybe if things don't work out with Dakota I'll try spending time with Georgie. Maybe I can fall in love with her, I just don't know.*

CHAPTER TWENTY

Wilt was lying in bed thinking about Dakota, Frank, and Georgie. One thing that came back to Wilt was Frank's comment about how the shooter knew Wilt, or how did she know that Wilt cared for Dakota. As far as Wilt knew, no one knew about Dakota. He tried to think of who Dakota told about them and their job hunting the shooter. He closed his eyes and tried to think back to the times when they talked to people.

Well let's see. The first time was at Billy the Kid's grave, and the shooter shot at me. All the people knew Dakota and I were together, but it was such a short time I don't think anyone would remember us. We talked to people when we were at the Coronado Historical Society building, but none of the Forest Service personnel would make that connection. The people we visited after the suspect tried to shoot me would not know anything about our relationship. No, I can't think of anyone who would link us together who we have met and talked to during our investigations. I'll think some more about it later.

The next day Wilt was up and ready to go to the hospital to see Dakota. He knew that the visiting hours were from eight am to eight pm except the ICU visiting hours were from 8 am to 8 pm. Wilt didn't know what floor Dakota was on and if she were still in ICU he could not see her until 10 o'clock. He called the hospital and was told Dakota Chavez was moved from ICU to regular care last night and was in room 515. He thanked the desk ambassador and got ready to go see Dakota.

Wilt walked into room 515 at the hospital and found Dakota was not alone. Frank Courts was with her and looked at Wilt with a surprised look on his face.

"Hello, Wilt. I've come to tell Dakota that her father and mother will be coming down from South Dakota this afternoon. I have suggested where they can stay for a day or two."

"That's nice Frank. Hello Dakota, how are you feeling?"

Dakota didn't look all that well and spoke very softly, "Hi Wilt. I understand you basically saved my life, thank you." She closed her eyes.

"We'll talk about that later, Dakota. I'm just happy that you are alive," Wilt said not knowing if Dakota heard him or not.

"Can we step out in the hall for a moment Wilt?" Frank said motioning his head toward the door.

Wilt was not quite sure how to act with Frank after their conversation yesterday. He didn't know if Frank was going to tell him that Dakota was off limits or what. "Yeah, sure," Wilt said.

Frank looked down at the floor and spoke softly, "I've been thinking about what you said yesterday about my judgement..."

"Look Frank, I said a couple of things..."

"Let me finish," said Frank rather forcefully. "You were correct to tell me that we will be back to square one if we cut you out of our investigation. I'd like to reinstate you and put you back on the case with a few stipulations."

"What stipulations?"

"First no one needs to know you are working with me on this case. Second you will report to me and only me, and third we both have to agree when and if Dakota is ready to resume her role in assisting you. I'm putting my career on the line here Wilt so don't let me down. Catch the shooter and all this negative stuff will probably go away."

"I could work this case independent of you Frank. That way you would not be risking your job."

"I really don't think the risk is very great because I have faith in you. Don't let me down."

They shook hands and walked back into the room to see Dakota. She seemed asleep so they didn't disturb her. Frank left to go back to the office and Wilt went to the waiting room so he could be there when Dakota was awake.

* * *

Helcom kept watching the front doors of every place she stayed on her trip from Wagon Mound. Any minute she expected the police to come in and ask for her, but it didn't happen.

She did the same thing when she checked into the Plaza Hotel in Las Vegas. No police around anywhere. Even in her room she kept looking out the window where she could see the main plaza and didn't see any police. She began to believe she had hit her target and escaped in what could have been a difficult situation.

When Helcom reached Albuquerque she immediately bought a newspaper. Looking at the bottom of the front page she found find an article about the shooting at Wagon Mound. The article was short and mostly about the car wreck and the male individual who was shot but it did mention Dakota Chavez by name who was a police officer. It also talked about the Medivac and that the shooter escaped.

OK, I can go to the hospital tomorrow and see how Dakota is. Anyone asks how I knew she was shot I 'll tell them that I read it in the newspaper.

The next morning Helcom called the hospital and found what room Dakota was in and that she could receive visitors. She dressed and drove over to the hospital. She arrived an hour after visiting hours began. As she was looking for a parking place she noticed Wilt Morrison walking to his car. She didn't want to be seen so she immediately pulled into an empty space.

Well, at least he will not be a problem being in the room when I visit. Wonder where he's going? No, I can't follow him I need to see Dakota and get her lowdown on what happened. Wonder if she thinks the shooter missed her heart intentionally or if it was just a bad shot?

Helcom found the right room and walked in. At first she didn't think Dakota recognized her, but in three seconds of staring at her Dakota had a look of recognition.

"Hello, uh, Helcom. How did you know I was in the hospital?"

"I read it in the paper. The article was about the shooting of some guy driving by, but it had the information about your being shot too. How are you doing?"

"My arm hurts like hell, but the doctors say I will have a full recovery. Just a matter of time."

"How long will you be in the hospital?"

"The doctor thinks I can probably go home tomorrow if I have someone to help me around the apartment. It's funny to see you. I just sent Wilt over to the complex to look you up and tell you that I was in the hospital. Room one eleven B, right?"

Damn he's going to find out that I don't live there. Got to think how I'm going to get out of this."

She tried to gather her thoughts, "Uh, my room number is one-ten B not one-eleven B, but it doesn't matter because I moved last week. I'm in another apartment complex not far from you."

"I should call Wilt and let him know that you moved."

"Did you see the person who shot you?" asked Helcom.

"That's a question that we want to ask," came a voice from a male standing behind Helcom.

Helcom turned around to see a rather large man with a badge in his hand looking at her. "My name is Frank Courts, Albuquerque PD. Who are you?'

"Helcom Garcia, just a friend who lives in the same complex as Dakota. I came to visit.'

"How'd you know she was here?" asked Frank.

Dakota spoke up, "She read it in the paper. I guess there is an article about the shooting in today's journal."

"Yes there is. Ms. Garcia do you mind if I talk to Dakota alone? It won't take long, and you can wait in the hall. Police business."

"I just wanted to know you were alright and I have some errands to run. I'll see you later, Dakota. I'm just glad you're OK.

Helcom walked out of the room surprised how good Dakota looked. She was not expecting her to be sitting up in bed wide awake and ready to carry on a conversation.

Her thoughts turned to Wilt. *What should I do about him knocking on the door to see if I'm home and find out I didn't live there?*

* * *

That morning Wilt got to the hospital the same time that visiting hours were allowed. He found Dakota awake and active.

"Hey Dakota, how are you this morning?"

"I'm sore as hell, but I'm glad I'm alive. I understand you played a big part in keeping me alive, thank you."

"I'm also the guy that sent you into harm's way, and I can't tell you how sorry I am."

"I didn't ask you why you thought the target was coming from the north, rather than the direction he actually came from."

"It came down to the line of fire. It was much easier to hit the target coming from the north, but I was wrong."

"I wonder if the shooter aimed for my shoulder rather than my heart. Do you think she intended not to kill me?"

"I think she knew time was a major factor and she just wanted to hit you anywhere that took you down. You were moving and she was in a hurry. I would not give her any credit for not killing you," Wilt added.

"That's just it, Wilt. When I heard the first shot I stopped and was looking up the hill when she shot. I'm convinced she could have killed me if she wanted to. That leads me to believe her targets were chosen for some reason as we suspected. I was not one of those chosen. She had to wound one of us so our attention would be diverted so she could escape."

"Well, maybe. I'm not convinced of that. Have you seen your parents yet?"

"No, they're still in route."

"All the police know about your wound. Is there anyone else I can notify for you?"

"There is one person I guess. The girl we met at the shooting range. She and I have talked once in a while. I think her name is Helcom and she lives in my apartment complex in room one-eleven B. Perhaps you could stop by and let her know where I am."

"I can do that when I leave. I talked to the doctor when I was coming up to see you. He is concerned that you will not be able to function without help for a while. I offer you my apartment where I can be there to assist you," Wilt said as he felt his heartbeat go a little faster.

"Thanks Wilt, but I talked to my parents, and they plan to stay in the area for at least one and maybe two weeks. They will be here to help me get used to living with one arm."

Wilt felt his anticipation disappear, "That's nice, Dakota. Well, I have a few things to do, and I understand Frank will be here shortly to ask you some questions."

"Thank you for coming by Wilt. I'll probably go home tomorrow afternoon. Will I see you tomorrow at my apartment? You can meet my parents."

"Sure. I'll call you before I leave the office."

"O.K."

Wilt felt like he should bend down and kiss her, but he didn't. He reached over and squeeze her good hand and felt her squeeze back. He left the room and walked down to his car. He left and headed for Dakota's apartment complex.

Once he reached the apartments he drove around to find the one hundred numbers. When he saw 111 he parked and walked upstairs to 111-B. There was no name on the name plate outside the door. He rang the doorbell. He waited 15 seconds and rang again. He could not hear any motion inside the apartment. He waited another 15 seconds and rang again. After another 15 seconds he deduced that Helcom was not home and started to leave. The door opened three doors down from 111 and Wilt caught up with the gentleman who came out of that apartment.

"Excuse me, sir. Do you know the lady that lives in one-eleven B?"

"Why are you asking?" responded the gentleman.

"A friend of the lady who lives there is in the hospital, and I was going to let her know."

"Sorry I don't know the people who live there. I just moved in a couple of weeks ago and don't know many people."

Wilt heard the word PEOPLE and asked, "Did you say people? Are there more than one?"

"I think there are two people that live in one-eleven. A guy and a gal. Don't know if they are husband and wife. That's all I can tell you," the guy said as he turned to go downstairs.

That's interesting, thought Wilt. *Dakota didn't mention anything about two people. Anyway, neither one is home.*

Wilt got back in his SUV and called Dakota. He told her there were two people that lived in 111- B, and neither were home. Dakota told Wilt that the address was wrong and should have been 110- B, not 111- B.

"It doesn't matter now anyway because Helcom came to see me and told me she moved to another apartment complex. She knows where I am so don't worry about it."

This was a waisted hour. Kind of strange that the girl would move out without telling Dakota goodbye. Maybe I should go back up and knock on 110- B, but Dakota told me her friend stopped by so she wouldn't be there anyway. Maybe I should check in the office to see if she lived there. Naw, a waste of time.

Wilt started his car and headed back to his office.

CHAPTER TWENTY-ONE

One of the most famous places in New Mexico besides Santa Fe is the Ghost Ranch, thought Helcom. *It was designated a National Natural Landmark by the National Park Service and was the home of Georgia O'Keeffe, the famous New Mexico painter. The 21,000-acre ranch would be a perfect place for a shooting. Doesn't matter who because it will get in the paper anyway. I must drive up there and pick out a place and an escape route. It's only about two hours north. I'll send my clue to the Police and maybe if I'm lucky Wilt will come up and try to find me.*

Helcom did drive up to Abiquiu, the small town that is next to the Ghost Ranch. She drove through the entrance to the ranch and was amazed at the beauty caused by various different colors of the large hills around the ranch. It didn't take her long to find a place where she had a view of the road for a few miles, and where she could not be seen. The problem was the exit plan. Helcom could not find a road out of the ranch other than the road she came in on. There were other roads around the ranch but generally they came back to the entrance road. She thought about using the entrance road and letting her target get further up the road before she shot so she could remain behind and do a quick exit. That caused problems of hitting the driver from behind the car.

Helcom drove out of the ranch through the single entrance. She noticed that up the main highway, which was State Highway 64, there was a deep arroyo that ran under the road. She drove up the arroyo until her car was out of sight from the highway. She walked across the hill back toward the entrance to the ranch. There were several large bushes covering the hill she was on.

There is my answer, she thought. *I can hide the car in the arroyo and walk back to where I can get a good view of the ranch entrance. I can shoot from there, hustle back to my car and drive away while people wonder why my target ran off the road. I think that will work. The only problem is I have to wait until someone drives through the entrance. It will work, and I know what my clue will be.*

* * *

Wilt Morrison's phone buzzed. He was sitting in the apartment with Dakota and her parents. They had been staying in Albuquerque for the last few days and were getting anxious to get back to South Dakota.

"Yeah Frank." Wilt said as he stood up and walked outside the front door.

"We have another clue, and it reads, **Some think it's haunted,**" Frank said.

"Jesus," exclaimed Wilt. "If I recall New Mexico has over four hundred haunted places around the state. But Dakota and I will take it on, and we'll see what we come up with. Thanks."

"How's Dakota doing?" asked Frank.

"She wants to go back to work. She can't shoot a rifle yet, but she wants to blow a hole in the shooter with that Three Fifty Seven

Magnum that she has. I told her it's not time yet and she would just be in the way."

"Sounds like her. Tell her hello for me and let me know what you can decipher."

Wilt walked back into the house and told Dakota about the latest clue.

"She went to Wagon Mound to get some attraction. Her next shooting will be somewhere really well known not only in New Mexico but also in the surrounding states. She wants press coverage so it can't be in the little places. What is really well known and has a lot of room for a sniper?" asked Dakota.

Wilt thought for a moment, "Let's quickly go down the major places that people say are haunted in New Mexico and see if any of them fit. We'll start with Albuquerque. There are basically two, one is Hotel Parq Central and the other is the KiMo Theater. Neither one is any fit for a shooter."

"What haunts them?" Dakota asked.

"Let's not go into that now. We can look up the history after we decide which one is our choice. Let's see, in Chama we have Foster's Hotel, which I can't see as a known site. In Cimarron there is the St. James Hotel. It could be the St. James Hotel because a lot of known outlaws stayed there. Let's put it down as a possibility."

"Wasn't it also a stop on the Santa Fe Trail. I think it's well known," added Dakota.

"Also, there's Dawson, which nothing is left there except a cemetery, but it's a possibility."

"Where's Dawson and why is it a possibility?" asked Dakota.

Many years ago, Dawson, which is seventeen miles from Cimarron, used to be a coal mining town. In nineteen thirteen there was an explosion in one of the mines and two hundred and fifty men were killed. I think it still is listed as the worst mine disaster in the U.S. if not the world. Again, in nineteen twenty-three another explosion killed one hundred and twenty-three men. In fact, the movie *Godless* was patterned after the Dawson mine disasters. The one big problem is that nothing is left there except a cemetery and it's hard to find. I think it's interesting but not conducive to sniper activity. Besides hardly anyone goes up there to see the cemetery. The rest of the active haunted places are down south around Cloudcroft, but none are famous or very large."

"What are we missing?" asked Dakota.

Wilt thought for a moment, "What place has ghosts around it and has enough room for a sniper shot? Hell, you need a farm or large park to set up a shot and also have an escape route. A farm? There is a farm in Moriarty, which is a town forty miles from Albuquerque, and it has a haunted farm, called McCall's Haunted Farm. Apparently old man McCall's original farmland stood in the way of the freeway when it was being built. McCall fought to save all his farmland but lost and had to destroy many of his crops. His family left and was never heard from again. Rumor has it McCall killed his family, and they haunt the farm. Most of the scary situations are set up and are props.

"Would that be a good place for a sniper?"

"I don't know. The Farm is only open in the evening and as I said It's more of a Halloween set up than having real ghosts. It's a possibility. Let me look at the surrounding area to see the potential escape routes."

"I'm really getting tired, Wilt. I can't think very straight right now.'

"I guess we can sleep on it. By-the-way did your friend come by again after she moved from here?"

"You mean Helcom? No, I haven't seen her again which is strange. But I didn't know her very well. She just seemed so lonely I felt sorry for her."

"Let's keep thinking about the haunted clue and I'll come by tomorrow. Say goodbye to your parents," said Wilt as he was walking out the door.

That's kind of strange about this Helcom girl. My curiosity is up, and I think I'll stop by the apartment office and see if Helcom left a forwarding address. I'll use my private investigator's badge to get the information.

Wilt drove around the complex until he found a sign for the office. He stepped in and was met by a nice-looking woman.

"May I help you?" she asked.

"Yes, ma'am. My name is Wilt Morrison and I'm investigating some shootings in the area. Can you tell me the forwarding address of a female that recently moved out of apartment one-ten B."

"Is this police business?" she asked.

"I'm not a police officer but I'm working with them. I'm a private investigator." He showed her his badge.

She looked at his badge and thought for a moment. "I don't think anyone has moved out of one-ten B. In fact, I know they are still there and have been there for a couple of years. What makes you think they've moved?"

"My partner, who lives in three twenty C is a friend of a lady named Helcom, who said she lived in one-ten B, but moved last week."

"Sorry I've never heard of this Helcom person, and I know no one moved out of one-ten B in the last week."

"Would you mind checking the records just so I can be sure?"

She rolled her eyes and said, "All right." She moved to a file drawer and her fingers walked through the files. "Here it is. The same couple is still in one-ten B, and no one is named Helcom."

"Since you are in the file would you check one-eleven B also, just to make I'm not confused about the address."

"The woman turned back to the file drawer, pulled one of the files and said, "The same couple has been in one-eleven B for the last three years. They're still there and none of them are named Helcom."

"Thank you ma'am. I appreciate your cooperation. Good day." He turned and walked out to his car.

On the way to his apartment his thoughts wandered to several areas. He thought of Dakota and how lucky he was that she was going to be all right. He wondered how she felt about him and if he should tell her about his feelings.

I'd tell her how I feel, but I'm not sure myself how I feel. I better start thinking about where the next shooter is going to be. McCall's Farm is interesting. I'll drive out there tomorrow and take a look at it.

The next day, after calling Dakota's parents to see how she was, Wilt drove out to Moriarty and took a look at McCall's Farm.

He called Dakota and told her that the land around the farm was too flat and there was no place to set up without being discovered. Plus trying to exit in a flat field is tricky at best. Even at night it would be a risk to do a shooting with that kind of terrain. He told her he scratched it off his list.

Wilt continued, "There are two other haunted events that are close. Wagner's Farmland Experience in Corrales is not necessarily haunted, but they do have a scary corn maze and some other things to do. But they are only open in September and October. The last thing was a ghost walk through Albuquerque Old Town. Many people have taken that guided walk at night and could hear strange things and enjoyed the stories the guide told. Again, it's not conducive to a sniper shoot."

Dakota was listening and said," The only ghost I have heard about before I came to New Mexico was the Ghost Ranch. I was studying Georgia O'Keeffe and she lived at that ranch. She painted a lot of pictures of the beautiful countryside and mountains."

"Damn," said Wilt. "That ranch is twenty-one thousand acres, enough space for an army of snipers. That has to be the area where the shooter is planning the next shot. I'll call Frank and head in that direction. If I can get there before she does maybe we can end this killing spree. It's worth a try. Thanks Dakota. I'll keep you informed."

"Frank, Dakota and I have decided the next shoot will be at the Ghost Ranch."

"That's interesting Wilt because the consensus here is it's going to be in Moriarty at the McCall's Haunted Farm. A lot of people visit that place which means there will be a lot of targets for the shooter any given evening."

"I went out there, Frank, and the flat fields and houses around the farm would scare me off. I don't think that's where she's going to be. The exit would be tricky."

"We're going to have police posted all over that area for the next few days. That's already been planned. Ghost Ranch isn't haunted. You might want to change your mind and join us."

"People say they can hear a man and a woman arguing at night next to a tree where one of the outlaws was hanged in the eighteen eighties. It's as haunted as most of the other places that claim ghosts," said Wilt. "Plus, as I said, there is plenty of room for a sniper to set up and escape."

"If I recall," said Frank. "There is only one road in and out of the ranch. The exit may be difficult."

"That's where she's going to be Frank. Mark my word."

"OK, Wilt. Good luck and be careful. I hope this works out for you because I'm getting a lot of pressure from above about your employment."

"It'll work out. I'm not worried about that," said Wilt sounding more confident than he felt.

CHAPTER TWENTY-TWO

Helcom left early in the morning and headed for the Ghost Ranch, which was 125 miles from Albuquerque. Just before Santa Fe she turned off on State Highway 285 and kept heading north. She went through the several Indian reservations including the Tesuque Reservation, the Pojoaque Reservation and also the Nambe Reservation.

As she passed the Nambe Reservation she thought, *One of these days I need to stop at the Nambe store. Nambe has been handcrafting high-quality, functional designs for the modern lifestyle. It was founded in 1951 when a metallurgist found an aluminum alloy and called it Nambe. They make simple, elegant designs. I love to stop in their shop in Albuquerque. But on to the task at hand.*

Before she passed through the San Juan Indian Reservation she took the State Highway 84 and continued north towards Abiquiu. She looked forward to seeing Abiquiu again because of its colorful mountains and canyons. Abiquiu is also a very popular filming destination for Westerns and other movies.

When Helcom reached the Ghost Ranch entrance she drove past and turned right into the arroyo she was in a couple of days before. After hiding her vehicle from the main road, she grabbed her gear and walked across the hill overlooking the ranch entrance.

She placed herself behind a large bush making sure she could not be seen from the main road, and from the road leading up to the buildings of the ranch. After orienting her rifle and scope she relaxed and waited for a visitor to enter the Ghost Ranch road. That visitor would become her target.

* * *

Wilt didn't know it, but he was thirty minutes behind Helcom. When he reached the entrance to the Ghost Ranch he stopped before turning to go onto the road. He noticed the road was straight, which meant the shooter could be in front of him waiting for him, or someone, to drive down the straightaway. He put his car in gear and drove his accelerator to the floor. The car leaped and started down the ranch road. Wilt swerved from right to left, left to right, abruptly stopped, and started again. He figured if the shooter were in the area she would be busy re-focusing her rifle sights because of his erratic movements. He continued his movements until he was covered by the ranch buildings. He didn't see anyone, and no one shot at him, so he turned around and did the same thing back to the main road. He drove two hundred yards from the entrance and pulled off to the side. He gathered his gear, which included his sniper rifle and other paraphernalia, crossed the road, and climbed the hill across from the ranch entrance so he could have a good view of the terrain. He selected a spot between some large brush. When the rifle was in place and the scope installed it was time to pull out his binoculars and start scanning the area looking for the shooter. Glancing up the ranch road and the hills on either side exposed no movement or person. After looking three or four times he began to wonder if his idea were wrong that the shooter would be in the area.

On his fifth sweep of the area with his binoculars he noticed a slight movement behind a large bush on the side of the hill across from him. He looked at that area for a few minutes and saw the movement again. Looking closely at the object that was moving he discovered it was the barrel of a rifle.

That's where she is! She's behind that large bush waiting for someone to turn into the entrance of the ranch. She would shoot from there rather than inside the ranch. This way she had a good exit. She must have parked her car in that arroyo behind her. I've got to stop her.

Wilt thought about getting behind her but that would take time. Any moment now someone could turn into the ranch entrance and get a bullet for their mistake. His only option was to shoot the rifle barrel. He thought of trying to shoot through the bush but there were too many branches that could deflect the bullet, plus he couldn't see the outline of her body because of the brush between them.

This is what you're trained for so get on it.

He looked through his scope, found the barrel, estimated the distance, focused, and slowly let out his breath. He hoped the barrel would not move and started putting pressure on the trigger of his sniper rifle. He heard a car slow down and start to pull into the ranch entrance. BLAM!

* * *

Helcom was getting tired lying on the ground trying not to move. She anticipated someone would turn into the ranch entrance before now. She had been lying there for over a half hour. She saw a car slow down and stop. She got ready to focus on the driver of the car when it suddenly sped up and started going back and forth across the road.

What the shit is the driver doing? She kept losing the car in her rifle scope, finding it, losing it again, then it would stop and start again.

The car stopped just long enough for Helcom to recognize the driver. *That's Dakota's partner the former sniper. He must have figured out the clue and is driving erratically because he knows I can't get a good shot with that movement.*

The car began to come back down the ranch road doing the same maneuvers. Helcom watched it until it got to the main road and turned north and disappeared.

What? He just drove off. I guess he figured since there were no shots I must be somewhere else. Good, I don't have to worry about him now.

She settled back down and once again sighted her rifle on the road just inside the entrance.

Time moved slowly for Helcom. It had been fifteen minutes, and no one had turned in the ranch entrance. She was getting a little impatient and started to move her rifle around slightly to look up the state road to see if any cars were coming. She told herself that she would give it twenty more minutes before leaving and go home. Feeling discouraged her mood changed when an oncoming car slowed down and started to turn into the road leading to the ranch. She cited in her rifle, estimated the speed of the car, and started to breath out and squeeze the trigger. All of a sudden there was a loud CLANG, and her rifle was jerked out of her hands followed by a rifle shot coming from across the street. Helcom's arms were tingling, and her right shoulder hurt.

What the hell? She wondered as she was trying to gather her thoughts. She grabbed her rifle and slid backwards further into the large bush she was next to. *That damn sniper came back and set up on the hill across the street. He probably has a Ghillie suit on so I can't see where he is.* Her thoughts turned to her rifle. *He hit the barrel so the thing may be ruined. At least it has to be recalibrated. I better get the hell out of here.* She grabbed her gear and got on her knees and was going to run to her car. *I need to start off and duck back behind the bush, run in a zig-zag pattern to my car. If I can just get over the edge of the arroyo I can duck down and get my car and make my escape* She took a deep breath, got on her feet, and ran. She ran first left, right, right again then left, each moment expecting a bullet to hit her. She reached the five-foot-high ditch dug by the water and ran to her car. She threw her gear in the back, moved the car to within fifty feet of the state road and stopped. She slammed on the accelerator and spun out to the road. Turning north she zig-zagged the car up the road. *Two can play this game. He hasn't shot at me yet so he's probably running down the hill to his car.* She spotted Wilt's car parked along the road. Slamming on the brakes and pulling out her handgun, she put down the passenger's window and pumped three rounds in the car's front tire. Once again the accelerator was smashed to the floor and the car jerked ahead.

* * *

Wilt heard the bullet hit the rifle barrel right after the sound of his rifle going off. Even with his head gear it was a loud noise. *Nice shot Wilt,* he thought. He glanced at the car that was entering the ranch and it had hesitated for a moment and went on up the ranch road. He injected another round in his weapon and his attention turned back to the shooter who he couldn't see behind the bush. Suddenly she bolted into plane sight running a zig-zag pattern in the direction away from the ranch road. Wilt tried to get a bead on her, but she was quick and disappeared into the arroyo before he could get off another shot. He grabbed his gear and started running down the hill toward his automobile. The shooter's SUV sped out of the arroyo and fish tailed on to the state highway. He stopped when he heard three pistol shots. He first thought maybe the shooter was shooting at him, but soon realized she was shooting his car. *Damn her. Now I have to change a tire while she speeds away, and there's no triple A out here!*

It took Wilt a half hour to change his tire. He was just leaving when he heard the siren coming up from the south. *I don't want to hang around and explain what happened here. I'll tell Frank when I get back to Albuquerque and he can straighten things out.* He turned his car around and headed south and passed the state patrol two miles from the entrance of the Ghost Ranch. Wilt knew the shooter could take several roads back to Albuquerque. She could take highway 95 through Heron Lake State Park, or the 112 to the 96 down toward Cuba and catch the 550 to Bernalillo and on the Albuquerque. The state police would have to spend too many resources to try and cover all the various ways to put up roadblocks. So, he would go on back to Albuquerque and start over. He did think he should call Frank and let him know what had happened. He waited until he had some good cell phone signals and put in the call.

"Frank, I told you she would be up here at Ghost Ranch."

"Well, did you get her?"

"No, she was too well hidden. I did shoot her rifle, though, but she got away from me by shooting the right front tire of my car."

"Her rifle?"

"Yes, that's all I could see of her because she was behind a large bush waiting for someone to turn into the ranch. After I hit her rifle she ran and jumped into a ditch caused by an arroyo where she was parked. By the time I got to my car she was gone."

"Couldn't you have gotten closer once you knew where she was?" asked Frank.

"I didn't have time because she was sighted in on the driver of a car. I had to shoot what I could see. How was the haunted Farm? Any shooters show up?" Wilt said sarcastically.

"It was a complete bust. I failed to notice that the Haunted Farm doesn't open until August 3rd, and we went down there on the 2nd. I caught a lot of shit for that mistake," he said, "The only conciliation is that you didn't get her either."

"No, but I'm getting damn close. Oh, by the way as I was coming back down from the ranch I passed a state patrol car with his siren on going toward the ranch. I didn't wait to explain what the shots were. I thought you would do a better job of that than I could."

"Yeah, thanks for that. Maybe it wasn't a call to the ranch. Could have been something else."

"I also wanted to get back to see how Dakota was doing. I'll see you in your office in the morning." Wilt noticed his phone signal was breaking up. He said in a loud voice, "If you can still hear me I'll see you in the morning," He clicked off. *I don't know why I shout when the signal on my phone is weak. The person on the other line can't hear me anyway.*

It took Wilt two and a half hours to get back to a service station near his condo. He showed the tire mechanic his flat tire and asked if it could be repaired. Since one of the bullets went into the sidewall, a new tire was purchased. He proceeded to Dakota's condo and spent an hour with her talking about his encounter with the shooter.

Dakota told him her parents were leaving in two days and she had to learn to get along alone.

"Well, I could help you with that problem. I have an extra bedroom which you could have if you wanted to move in with me?"

Dakota looked at Wilt, "I don't know, Wilt. I believe I can manage here. It's the dressing and undressing that I have to practice. I don't think you would be much help in that area."

Wilt felt his face getting flush, "But I could cook for you and take you back and forth to the office. We'd have more time to discuss our strategy and plans."

"Let me think about it. I just think I would be more comfortable here, even with the dressing problems."

"Suit yourself. But the offer is still on the table if you change your mind," he said a little deflated.

* * *

Helcom knew Wilt would not be able to follow her until he changed the tire. She was concerned about him possibly calling in the State Patrol and trying to get them to respond but there were too many roads back to Albuquerque to try and block them all. As she drove she started thinking about what had just happened.

I have to do something about Morrison. He's getting too close and almost had me this time. I need to figure a way to eliminate him, and once that's done, do the same with his partner Dakota. I need to send him some kind of clue and draw him out where he is not expecting me to be. First I probably need to get a new rifle because of the bullet hitting the barrel. She kept thinking and an idea came to her. She just needed to put the details on it, but it might work.

When she arrived back at her house it was time to take a good look at the damage done to her rifle. Just as suspected the barrel was slightly bent where it had been hit. As she wondered how to replace her weapon she rubbed her sore shoulder.

The only way I can think of to fix this rifle is to get another one, but that costs money. I could go to a title company and put my car up as collateral and get the rifle, but then how would I get my car back? I could pull a steak out on Dakota's apartment and break in and take her rifle when she's at the hospital. That would be risky with all the people that live in that complex. I could sell my small car to a car company and have a new rifle but only one car, plus I bet the police would be looking for a cash deal for a car. They may also be looking at gun stores for a sniper rifle purchase. I guess I'd better go back to El Paso to get this deal done.

Since she was going to end up with one car, she decided to go to a title store and get cash for her title for her small car. There were a number of "title for car "companies in Albuquerque that she figured the police would not think of checking all of them. After a set time the title company would possess the car and sell it for the loan payback.

Once that was done she would drive to El Paso and purchase an appropriate rifle. This part of the plan was set. All she had to do now was lay low for a short period of time before acting on her plan. In the meantime, another plan was forming in her head on how to get rid of Morrison.

Helcom knew that Albuquerque was well known for its balloon fiesta. She noticed the other morning that eight or nine hot air balloons were in the air over Rio Rancho. She started thinking about how she could lure Morrison to get in a balloon where she could shoot him in the air. She considered getting in a balloon herself, but the escape plan would be difficult. Plus trying to hold the pilot captive while in the air would be difficult and very risky. She could not stop thinking about how she could put this plan together and still escape to continue shooting. With Morrison out of the way she thought she could still kill people who deserved it, and the police would have difficulty catching her.

The next day Helcom drove to El Paso. She stopped at a car title company but because she was out of state they would not do business with her. She drove back to Las Cruces and tried again. The negotiation went smoothly but the car title company didn't' give her the cash she wanted. It was enough to purchase a rifle, but only about half of the value of the car. They gave her twenty days to bring the car in or they would take possession of the vehicle.

Her next stop was a gun shop in the same town. She walked out with a new Daniel Defense Delta 5 Pro. This rifle uses 308 ammunition like her other rifle, and the scope on the old rifle would fit the new one. Her next step was to sight in the new rifle, then start planning her attack. She drove home satisfied with herself and the plan that was forming in her mind.

The next day Helcom went to the shooting range and shot at the steel targets which were 750 yards out. The first few shots were high, so she adjusted her scope until she was satisfied with her shots. OK *Morrison, I'm ready, all I have to do now is get you to be the target.*

CHAPTER TWENTY-THREE

Wilt Morrison was visiting Dakota at her condo. "I'm still curious why your friend, what's her name,..

"Her name is Helcom," said Dakota. "It's a hard name to forget. Just think of your father saying Hell, *here comes another daughter* and you will remember her name."

"OK, anyway I still wonder why she said she lived in your complex when she didn't."

"I don't know. Maybe she was just trying to be friendly. Maybe she was staying with someone and didn't want the complex to know about it."

"Maybe she wanted to get to know you and know more about plans to stop the shooter. Lots of maybes. I still don't like it. I may drive out to the shooting range and talk to her."

Dakota said, "She told me she shoots at the range but only uses a small caliber pistol. She didn't even know what my rifle was when I told her what I had."

"I don't know why I'm curious, but I'm going to trust my instincts and I think something is weird about her. I'll be back to see how you are doing. Want to move in with me yet?"

"Thanks, but I'm doing just fine right here."

"Suit yourself, see you later."

Wilt drove out to the Albuquerque shooting range. It was mid-morning and the range had not been open long. He parked in front of the office and walked in.

"Morning," the clerk said half looking at Wilt.

"Morning. I'm looking for Helcom, is she here?"

"Why do you want her?" asked the clerk.

Wilt was a little taken back by the question and hesitated for a moment. "I know she shoots here once in a while, and I thought maybe I could join her in a shoot. I understand she uses small caliper pistols."

'You can't hit the steel targets with a small caliber pistol," the clerk mentioned.

"She shoots at the steel targets?" Wilt asked somewhat surprised.

"Been doing that since she came out here. Spent most of her life hunting and shooting and is quite good at it. In fact, she just bought a new rifle and tried it out this morning."

Wilt thought, *I wonder if she bought a new rifle because her barrel was bent from my bullet.*

"She say why she bought a new rifle?"

"Nope, and I didn't ask her."

"Can you tell me where she lives?" asked Wilt.

"I can, but I won't," replied the clerk. "I don't know who you are or why you want her address, but sorry, you're not getting it from me."

Wilt tried to explain who he was and why he wanted to talk to her. He pulled out his P.I. credentials and showed them to the clerk, but the clerk would not budge about giving him the information.

"Get something legal or bring the cops out with you and then you can get her address."

"OK. I might do that." He turned and left.

On his way back Wilt called Dakota. He started talking as soon as she answered. "I found out that your friend Helcom target shoots at the steel targets with a sniper rifle. I don't think she is an innocent little thing who doesn't know weapons."

"Really. She just called and asked me if she could come over and visit for a while."

"What did you tell her?"

"That I was still hurting and maybe she could visit next week when I felt better."

"You think she agreed to that?" asked Wilt.

"I don't know. She said she was taking a hot air balloon ride in the morning and maybe she'd come by tomorrow afternoon."

Wilt had seen the hot air balloons in the air lately. Some of the balloon operators would practice for the upcoming Albuquerque Balloon Festa which took place around the first week in October. They would go up in the morning when it was cool. Some offered individual rides, and other companies such as Rainbow Riders, who had several large balloons, could take up to ten or fifteen people on each ride.

Wilt thought for a moment. He didn't want Dakota to be in danger in case Helcom decided to visit her this afternoon anyway. No telling what she might do to Dakota. "I'm going to come by and discuss this new situation with you. I'll be there in twenty minutes."

He called Frank Courts at his police office. "Frank, I think I have a new lead on our shooter. Her name is Helcom Garcia. I need to know where she lives so I can pay her a visit."

Frank said, "Just a minute and let me look." A half minute went by, "There are a bunch of H. Garcias who live in and around Albuquerque so this may take a while."

"I don't know how much time we have, but I think she's who we are looking for. I just finished visiting the shooting range and found out that she has a sniper's rifle and shoots steel targets. Wait, the main clerk at the range told me he knew her address but would not give it to me. He said he needed something legal or a police officer to ask and he'd let them know. Could you send an officer out there if necessary and get the address that way?"

"Yeah, no problem. There are usually several officers at the police range that's out there next to the civilian range. I'll see what I can do."

"Thanks Frank. Let me know what you find." Wilt clicked off.

He started thinking about Dakota and her relationship with Helcom Garcia. *If this Helcom woman wanted to find out what we knew about the shooter one way to do that was to befriend Dakota or me. Based on what I know, Dakota didn't tell her much about what we knew. The other interesting thing is when she shot Dakota up at Wagon Mound she aimed just above and left of the heart. I don't know if she did that intentionally or because Dakota wasn't moving and Helcom could of had a kill shot. I don't want to take the chance that Helcom gets another opportunity. I have to convince Dakota to move in with me so I can keep an eye on her. I'm not fooling myself any because I do care for her, probably more than I should.*

Wilt drove up to Dakota's condo, got out of his car and knocked on Dakota's door. It took half a minute before she opened the door.

"Wilt, what a surprise. You could have told me you were coming."

"I'm sorry Dakota, but I have had too much on my mind to think of everything. Can I come in?"

"Of course," said Dakota a little embarrassed about not asking him in.

Wilt explained to Dakota about what he learned about Helcom. Dakota was surprised.

"You mean she shoots at the steel targets?" explained Dakota.

"Yes, and she has a new sniper rifle because I believe her other rifle's barrel is crooked from my shot."

"And I actually spent time with her and didn't know any of this. Do you think she tried to be my friend to find information about our plans?" asked Dakota.

"No question in my mind. The real problem is now that we are on her trail there is no question that I think she may be stalking you. That's why she wanted to know where you live."

"What does she gain by stalking me?"

"She finds information about me, who is her main threat. If she takes us both out she thinks her problems are solved." Neither one said anything for a moment. "I really think it would be wise if you stayed with me at my condo. You would be safer, and I wouldn't have to worry so much about you. I'm serious about this Dakota. I don't want anything to happen to you because I care about you. It's more than you being my partner, I want our relationship to be deeper than that."

Dakota was silent for a moment. She just stood in front of Wilt and looked at him. She slowly walked toward him and put her right arm around his neck and kissed him. It was a long, lingering, wet kiss which surprised Wilt. After a second he realized what was happening and started to put both arms around Dakota, but stopped and let his right arm hang down by his side because he didn't want to hurt her wound. He held her against him and felt himself getting aroused.

She moved her head back, looked up at him and said, "Is that deep enough?"

"That was very nice," Wilt said feeling his heart racing. "I hope there are many more of those coming my way. Can I take your actions as a YES you are coming over to my condo?"

"I'll go to your condo because I want to, not because I think it's safer. Besides what will keep Helcom from getting at me there?"

"Well first of all I don' t think she knows where I live, and I'd like to keep it that way. Second, I plan to keep her so busy concerned for herself she won't have time to be worried about you."

"Let me put a few things together and we can go in fifteen or twenty minutes. What about Georgie?

"I haven't talked to Georgie for a while. I think our relationship has turned into a friendship more than anything else."

Dakota talked as she was throwing things into a suitcase, "I wonder if she would agree with that."

"I hope so," said Wilt.

Thirty minutes later Dakota and Wilt walked out of her condo and Wilt put her things in the trunk. Before he entered his car he stood outside and looked all around the parking lot. He didn't see anyone sitting in their car. As he left he kept his eyes on the rearview mirror for anyone who may be following them. He saw no one suspicious.

"Am I sleeping in the spare room?" asked Dakota.

"That would be the best for your arm, but not necessarily the best for me."

"We'll see how it goes, but it will be a while before I can move into your bedroom."

Things went as expected and Dakota put her things away in the small closet and the chest of drawers that were available. Before Wilt ordered from the local Italian Restaurant for delivery he asked Dakota what she wanted. When that was settled he offered her a glass of wine and they both sat down and looked at each other from across the small living room.

"So, what's your plan Wilt?"

"Once I find where she lives I'll see if Frank can provide a watch on her house. I will be the person who follows her until she is ready to strike again. Once she sets up for another kill we'll will move in, and it will be over."

"Sounds simplistic to me. She has outsmarted us so far. How do you know it will be that easy?"

"I don't know, but I don't have another plan. We could ask for a search warrant, but I don't think she would keep any incriminating evidence in her house."

"You may not have enough evidence to warrant a warrant." Said Dakota.

"You may be right. Any ideas?'

Dakota thought for a moment, "Where do you think she keeps her rifle?"

"If it's not in her house it's probably at the shooting range where she works."

Wilt took his phone off the table where he left it and called Frank Courts. When Frank answered Wilt said, "Has any officer talked to the clerk at the shooting range yet?"

"No," said Frank. "Officer Clark should be over there is an hour, why?"

"Would you ask the officer if the clerk knows if Helcom keeps her rifle at the range or takes it home."

"No problem," said Frank. "I'll let you know. You can tell me why the question later."

The doorbell rang. "Must be our dinner," said Wilt.

After dinner and a nice long kiss, they both retreated to their respective rooms and said good night.

* * *

Helcom decided it was time to take a chance and eliminate both Dakota and Wilt Morrison. She was convinced once they were out of the picture her chances of getting caught by the regular police was much less. She had devised a plan to get rid of Morrison which was a little complicated but killing Dakota was easy. She would put a silencer on her forty-five caliper Glock handgun and shoot her in her apartment. Obviously, Dakota would let her inside her dwelling because she knew her. She figured no one would find her for a few days especially if she got rid of Morrison the next day.

Helcom drove over to the condo where Dakota lived. She noticed her car was in the parking lot so she much be home. She put her Glock in her purse and walked to Dakota's apartment. She knocked on the door a few times, but no one answered. She was about to leave when a woman came out of the room next door.

"She's not home, which I guess you know by now. She left with her suitcase and some hanging cloths with a man."

"Thanks," said Helcom. "How long ago did she leave?'

"About twenty minutes ago. I would guess she was going to stay a while."

Helcom got back into her car and sat a minute thinking. *She probably went with Morrison. I guess it's time to implement my plan and at least get rid of Morrison. I can get Dakota later. Her car is still here probably because she doesn't want to drive with her left arm in a sling.*

Helcom drove over to Wilt Morrison's office building. She parked in the lot across the street from the office. It was getting dark but there were enough lights that she could see as she walked to the building. She found his office which was listed on his internet site and slipped a note under his door. As she left she looked around and didn't see anyone. Satisfied she had not been spotted she got in her car and drove home.

CHAPTER TWENTY-FOUR

Wilt left his condo the next morning while Dakota was still sleeping. He drove to downtown Albuquerque and parked in his usual spot. He walked to his office, unlocked the door, and stepped inside. He noticed an envelope on the floor, just inside the door. He retrieved a letter opener from his office, got down on one knee and gently lifted one end of the envelope and looked to see if there was any powder or anything else under it. Seeing nothing he gently lifted the envelope and put it on his desk. Slowly he slid the letter opener into the top of the sealed envelope and ran it across the top. Satisfied that there was nothing dangerous inside, he took out the note and read the message. It was hand printed and read: THIS IS THE NEXT CLUE: UP UP AND AWAY – 5 AM FRIDAY MORNING. NO POLICE.

Wilt stood looking at the message. *What the hell? This has to be from Helcom. She is sending me a clue to her next shooting, but it's only for me. No Police? Up Up and Away are lyrics to the song My Beautiful Balloon. She wants me to take a hot air balloon ride at five am on Friday morning. We're going to see who is the best sniper by shooting at each other while riding in a hot air balloon? We'll see who can determine the angles of the moving balloon in the air and adjust our sights to the target. What about shooting through the basket?*

What about shooting the propane canister used to fuel the heater which would explode killing the rider?. What about shooting the flame heaters that control the rise and fall of the balloon? Friday is two days away. We need to find where she lives and take her out before this crazy idea actually happens.. I better call Dakota and discuss this with her.

Dakota was up and having a cup of coffee when the phone rang. Wilt told her he had received the next clue and had to talk to her about it. He said he would come right home because he wanted her ideas and there wasn't much time.

Wilt made a call to a friend of his that has a hot air balloon. After explaining to him what was going down, his friend was willing to assist Wilt in this adventure. Wilt drove to his condo and showed Dakota the note he found.

After Dakota read the note she said, "You're not going to challenge her are you? Have you ever tried to shoot someone in a hot air balloon? Where did she get this idea?"

"I assume you have heard of the Albuquerque Balloon Fiesta?"

"I've heard of it but have never been to one. Is it a big deal?"

"Each year balloonist from all over the world come to Albuquerque to participate in this Balloon Fiesta. Last year there were five hundred and fifty balloons all in the air at the same time. It is a spectacular scene. You also have a half mile of tents set up in a row selling various items and food. More than a half million people come to this event in the week that it is open. It always starts the first Saturday of October and runs each day until the second Sunday. Right now, a month before the event, each morning you will see a dozen or so balloons in the air getting ready for the Fiesta."

"Wilt, the best thing you can do is to alert the police and have them pick her up before she gets in the air. Don't do this alone, please."

"I would just as soon not participate in something like this but if we can't find her at home it may be our only chance to end the random urban shooter."

'If she knows where you are why can't she just shoot the balloon down by shooting holes in the material that holds the air?" asked Dakota.

"That's called the envelope," said Wilt. "Most envelop material is made of Nylon and polyester. If it gets a tear in the material it will not spread. It would take a hell of a lot of bullets to take down a balloon by putting little holes in it."

"So, what's the best way?"

"The best way to take down a balloon is to shoot the pilot or try to hit the propane canister that fuels the burner. Most times it will explode if hit with a high caliber bullet. You could also try and hit the burner which the pilot uses to raise and lower the rig," said Wilt.

"How do you lower it? I thought you could only control the upward motion of a hot air balloon," asked Dakota.

"Hot air keeps the balloon rising until the air starts to cool. The burner is used to put more hot air in the envelope and make rise. When the pilot wants to land he lets the air cool, so it starts to descend. He controls the speed of the descent by putting a little hot air in the envelope as it descends to slow it down. A good pilot can make a nice soft landing."

"What about the thing that holds the people? Can it stop a bullet?" asked Dakota.

"It's called the basket or gondola. No, not normally because most are made of wicker or rattan. A bullet would go right through the sides of the basket, so they don't offer that type of protection," answered Wilt.

"So, it's going to be whoever sees who first and gets the first shot will win this stupid dual?" said Dakota.

"Depending on what or who they hit. It won't be easy to hit a target that is moving laterally and upward at the same time. Besides, I have an ace up my sleeve," said Wilt.

"Just what are you talking about?"

"I have a friend that wanted to build a hot air balloon that the police could use as an observation platform. To reflect any rounds shot at the basket he put a one-inch-thick band Kevlar all around the inside of the basket. He also protected the burners by putting Kevlar around them. The fuel canister was also behind the Kevlar band, so it was protected. As far as I know it was the only balloon outfitted this way. Helcom doesn't have a chance if we can find her and destroy her and the balloon she's in. For extra protection we will also have bullet proof vests on."

"Doesn't that make the balloon to heavy with all that Kevlar?" said Dakota.

"No. It's just like having an extra person in the basket. You only go up with a few passengers."

"Did the police buy it?" asked Dakota.

"No. About that time the idea of using drones for air observation became popular."

"Is your friend available and willing to take this risk?"

"Yes. I called him before I left the office this morning and he is willing to help," said Wilt.

"What's my role in this?" asked Dakota.

"Can you drive a car with your shoulder in a cast?" asked Wilt.

"I can hold the steering wheel at the bottom with my cast hand and the top with my good hand. Yes, I can maneuver a car with no problem. Why?"

"We're going to be in the air, and someone needs to follow us and help with the landing. There will also be some other cars and pickups helping so you will not have to get out of the car and pull on the ropes," said Wilt. "These people are called Chasers and are an important part of the balloon system. They hold the balloon in place while it gets air and gas, and they help stable the balloon on the landing. I'll need a ride after I bring down Helcom. Also, I hate to say it, but I may need a witness in case my plan doesn't work."

"Your plan better work. I'm not ready to lose you because I'm beginning to really like you," said Dakota.

"We also need to drive out and find where we will be getting the balloon ready. We'll do that in the morning," said Wilt.

"Where it is?" asked Dakota.

"It's a practice area. The actual Fiesta takes place at the area behind the Balloon Museum off of Alameda Blvd. We'll drive south on Unser Boulevard and get on Paseo Del Norte and turn right. There is plenty of space out there for balloons go up and land. We'll find my friend there so we can practice."

"By the way, what's his name?" Dakota asked.

"Richard Bradford," replied Wilt.

"You going to tell me how to get a balloon in the air?" said Dakota.

"I'll show you that in the morning and keep you informed as things progress," said Wilt. "You have any more questions?"

"Just one. Do we have Helcom's address yet?"

"That's a good question. Let me call Frank and ask him." Wilt pulled out his phone and hit Frank's number. The answering machine told Wilt to leave a message. "Frank, Wilt. Do you have Helcom's address yet? It's important we get it soon so we can go pick her up. Please call me back."

* * *

Helcom was in the middle of writing a note to whom it may concern when her phone rang. She didn't recognize the number right away and almost ignored it, but it suddenly came to her that it was where she worked. "Hello," she said.

"Helcom this is George at the range. I just wanted you to know that there was a private detective in here this afternoon asking where you lived. I didn't tell him, but then later an Albuquerque detective arrived and asked the same questions. I had to give him your address from our employee records. Don't know what they wanted and didn't ask. Just thought I'd let you know."

"Thanks George," and she clicked off. *So, they think they know who I am and what I have been doing. I better take my gear and go to a hotel room for the night and lay low until Friday morning.*

She pulled into a hotel, got a room for two nights and finished the note she was writing.

This note is in case I get caught or killed during my fight with Morison. People need to know what I have been doing and why. They also need to know why women should be accepted in a military sniper's school.

The note read: **To Whom it may concern: I am the Sniper who has been shooting people all over New Mexico. All but one of the people who were my targets deserved to die. They were** either cheating on their wives, or selling drugs, or not paying taxes, or doing some other nefarious activity. I wanted to prove that women should be allowed into military sniper's school. Women can be excellent shots and take as much physical pain as men. I think I have proved my point. The stupid military is WRONG!!

She put the note in her pocket knowing she would destroy it later if necessary, or it would be found when they examined her body. She was confident she would live to destroy it.

She had one more thing to purchase to be used on Friday morning. She knew where she would get it and walked out the door. When her purchase was accomplished she returned to her hotel room and placed it with the rest of her equipment that she brought into the room. She turned on the TV in her hotel room, made sure her equipment was secured to the bed with locks, and went out to eat.

When Helcom returned to her hotel room she started planning for the next day. *I'll drive out to the practice area and watch the balloons go up. I don't think there will be more than a dozen. I will stay back so no one will spot me and find the balloon that Morrison will be in on Friday. I'm sure he will be there with some friend, and they will practice putting the balloon in the air. It will be easy to determine which balloon he will be in.*

* * *

The clock alarm went off at three thirty in Wilt's room. The alarm wasn't really necessary because he'd been awake most of the night thinking about the coming morning. He got out of bed and put on the coffee. He remembered the time before he went to bed. He and Dakota were in his living room discussing the next day.

"I really wish you would not go through with this," Dakota said.

"I don't want to, but I think I must. If I don't and someone else is shot it would seem to be my fault."

"What about us, Wilt? Do you think we have a future together?" asked Dakota.

"I would like to think so. Two things we could do. One is to form our own agency, and the second is to become lovers," said Wilt. "If we form an agency you may have to work as a police officer until we get things going. We would probably need the income."

'I know what we have to do to become lovers," said Dakota smiling.

"I could become very fond of you Dakota. In fact, I think I already am."

"Since this might be your last evening, I would like to sleep with you tonight," Dakota said in a hesitant voice.

The next morning after Wilt put on the coffee he went back into his bedroom and touched Dakota on the arm. "Hey kiddo, it's time to arise and shine. By the time you get dressed the coffee will be ready."

She turned toward him, smiled, and said, "Last night was very nice. I hope we have many more."

"We will, trust me," was Wilt's response.

By four o'clock they were in Wilt's SUV headed for the practice area.

"Why so damned early?" asked Dakota.

"As you know the balloon is raised by hot air. The ambient air in the morning is cool so there is a big difference between the air inside the balloon and on the outside. As the day goes on it gets warmer and thus more heat is needed to keep the balloon in the air. In early fall, mornings are best for balloon rides."

They both fell quiet as they drove along the road. It was getting lighter as the sun was coming up behind them over the Sandia Mountain. Wilt slowed down as they reached their destination. He started looking for Richard Branford's pickup and his balloon crew. When he saw Richard he pulled off the road into an open area and parked next to the other cars as he knew they would be out of the way of the rising balloon. Once out of the car he greeted Richard and the rest of the crew and introduced Dakota to everyone. He started to look around at the other balloons that were being readied for their trip. He was looking for Helcom, but he knew she would probably be someplace close by but far enough away not to be seen. He also thought she would also be looking for him. Wilt took out his camera and took pictures of all the balloons at the practice site. *I need to memorize the different colors and designs on each practice balloon so if I see one tomorrow that is not one of these then I'll know it's the balloon carrying Helcom.*

The five-man crew started to spread out the envelop on the ground. The average balloon is fifty to sixty feet wide and seventy to eighty feet tall. Two men were spreading out the balloon and two men were hooking it up to the basket or gondola. They turned the gondola on its side facing the balloon and started a large fan blowing air into the balloon. It took ten minutes to fill the balloon with air. Bradford started the burners attached to the gondola directing the flame toward the open mouth of the balloon. In a few minutes, the balloon started to lift. As it lifted it pulled the gondola upright. Bradford and Wilt jumped into the gondola as it started to be lifted by the balloon. The whole thing was almost lifting off the ground.

The crew were holding on to ropes attached to the basket not letting the balloon lift.

"Are you going up?" Dakota yelled to Wilt trying to he heard over the balloon noise.

"We will tomorrow," yelled Wilt back. "I just wanted to see the basket layout, so I'll know what I'm getting into." After five minutes he jumped out of the gondola.

"I'll take it for a little ride," said Bradford as another man climbed in the gondola. 'If you want you and Dakota can go with the chasers."

"Let's get in the car," Wilt said. "This is what I want you to do tomorrow. Chase the balloon."

As the balloon lifted and started to climb, it also moved in an easternly direction.

"The horizontal movement of the balloon is controlled by the different winds at various levels. The pilot studies the wind directions prior to launching and knows how to maneuver the balloon in the desired direction by rising to a certain height where the wind will take him where he wants to go," said Wilt.

"Does he have maps in the gondola?" asked Dakota.

"They used to have maps. Now they have a laptop that give them a picture in real time of where they are and where they want to go. It also highlights high voltage wires, which are the nemesis of balloon pilots."

"OK, I only have one last question. How do they land?" asked Dakota.

"As the air in the balloon cools, the balloon drops. In order to slow the downward movement if it drops too quickly the pilot activates the burner for a few seconds putting hot air into the envelope to slow the drop speed. A good pilot will be able to put the gondola on the ground with minimum landing force, so no passenger gets injured," said Wilt.

"There's a lot more to flying a hot air balloon than I thought," said Dakota.

As Wilt looked at her, his phone buzzed. It was Frank Courts. "Wilt, we got the address of the shooter, but no one is home. I have asked for a search warrant so we can see if there is any evidence inside the house. It's will take a while, but I'll get back to you as soon as we have some news."

"Thanks Frank."

"Where are you and what are you doing?"

Wilt thought for a moment, "I suspect Helcom may use a hot air balloon for her next target. Just a guess. I'm out here with Dakota giving her a lesson on balloon flying."

"What gave you this idea? Did you get a clue or something?"

"Keep me informed about what you find in the house, please."

"I asked you if you got some information."

"Sorry Frank we're in a bad reception area, you're fading out. Sorry," and he clicked off.

Wilt decided to take a drive around the area to see if he could locate the balloon that Helcom would be in. He and Dakota could not see any other balloons except the ones in the practice area.

"This is really puzzling that there aren't any other balloons in the area," said Wilt.

"She must have some friend that has a balloon some other place and will bring it or fly it over in the morning," said Dakota.

"'We best get here early to see if we can spot the balloon she's in. I hate for her to get the first shot and not know where it's coming from."

"I still wish you'd call this whole thing off," pleaded Dakota.

"Too late now. I'll be just fine, you'll see," said Wilt with less confidence than he displayed.

* * *

Helcom drove out near the balloon practice area early that morning. She made sure she parked her car where it could not be seen from the road. She brought her strong binoculars along and slowly walked to where she could see all around the practice area. She counted twelve crews getting the envelope's set out on the ground. It took her a few minutes to spot Wilt and Dakota. Helcom first noticed Dakota who had her left arm still in a sling. The balloon where Wilt and Dakota were standing started to Inflate and straighten up. Helcom took out her camera and took a picture of the design on the envelope so she could memorize it. She put her gear away and slowly backed off the small hill she was on and walked back to her car.

When she reached the hotel room she immediately opened her laptop and turned to the weather forecast. She paid attention to the direction and speed of the winds, both at ground level and at higher altitudes. She knew that once the balloon was in the air it would fly in the direction the wind was blowing. As it rises it will catch the second wind and go that direction. She plotted where the balloons should be in the first minutes in the air, and then changed the position as the time passed and the balloons got higher. Satisfied, she once again secured her gear and went back to bed and tried to get some more sleep.

* * *

Wilt and Dakota didn't do much the rest of the day. That evening they went out for an early dinner and came back and went to bed. Neither one slept much and were ready to get out of bed when the alarm went off at three am. They were both quiet getting dressed and Dekota scrambled some eggs as Wilt double checked his gear. He knew it was going to be a little cramped in the gondola with the two propane canisters and the two riders, the sniper's rifle, binoculars, and extra magazines filled with rounds. He also figured the bullet proof vests they were both wearing would make it more difficult to maneuver around the gondola. Wilt was determined to find Helcom as quickly as he could and end this "balloon dual" as he called it.

On the way to the practice area Dakota took and squeezed Wilts' hand. He looked at her and she had tears in her eyes. He squeezed her hand and took a deep beath.

"I'll do what I need to do, Dakota. I know you understand that."

"I love you Wilt. I'm really worried about what may happen."

"I know you are. I'm going to do my best to come back to you. I realize I love you too. I want our lives to continue because I know we will both be happy for a long time. I know you can't help it, but please don't worry and just keep your eyes on our balloon so you and the crew can pick us up after we finish."

They reached the takeoff area just as their crew was spreading out the envelope. Wilt parked the car and moved toward Dakota and gave her a long kiss. He picked up his gear and walked to the launch area. He took a few minutes to look at the horizon all around him determined to see the balloon that would carry Helcom. He didn't see any other balloon anywhere. He put on his bullet proof vest.

Some balloon will appear from some direction as soon as we get in the air. He also knew that no other balloons were at the practice area

221

because Richard told them what was going on this morning, and it would be best if they either skipped the day or lifted off later.

There wasn't much chatter between crew members as they readied the balloon. When the envelope was full and started to rise, Wilt picked up his gear and walked toward the gondola. When the crew stabilized the balloon Wilt put his gear in the gondola and climbed in. As soon as he was in, Richard also climbed in. They both got organized and Richard pulled the rope activating the burner. He let it burn for ten seconds and waited. Noticing that the balloon was starting to rise, he opened the burner for another ten seconds, then another ten seconds until the balloon was about one hundred feet off the deck and drifting with the lower wind. The crew, including Dakota, climbed in their cars and looked for routes to chase the balloon.

Wilt kept looking for the other balloon. *I still don't see any other balloon in the air. Maybe she changed her mind. Wouldn't that be something!*

The balloon was two hundred feet and Wilt was still looking at the horizon when suddenly a bullet came through the bottom of the gondola and ricocheted off the steel canister between Wilt and Richard and continued out of the gondola. The sound of the shot reached their ears.,

"Holly shit," exclaimed Wilt. "She's on the ground shooting up at us." He immediately looked down over the edge of the gondola but could not see where she was. He yelled at Richard, "It's just a matter of time before a bullet gets one or both of us or hits the propane canister and we blow up. Take us up as quickly as you can."

Richard pulled on both ropes and both burners went off at the same time. As the balloon started up another bullet came through the floor and landed in Richard's upper shoulder. Richard yelled, let go of the burner ropes and fell to the floor wincing in pain. Wilt pulled out his phone and called Dakota.

When she answered he said, "Dakota, Helcom is on the ground somewhere shooting us through the floor. Richard has already been hit. I can't find her. Can you help us?"

Dakota felt her heart jump and insulin flow through her body. "Shit. What can I do? I didn't bring my rifle. I don't see her either."

"Another bullet just came through here and bounced off the propane canister. We could blow up with the next fucking shot. Just be creative and do what you can."

Dakota dropped her phone in the passenger's seat and turned her car around with one hand on top of the steering wheel and her other holding the bottom. She started looking at the area below where the balloon was flying.

She thought she saw a puff of dust come up from a spot fifty yards away from the road. She heard Wilt over her open phone.

"Damn, that's the forth shot. That one grazed my lower right leg. It's just a matter of time."

Dakota made a quick decision and dropped the gear shift lever to a lower gear. She drove toward the dust spot, she saw another puff come up and heard Wilt yell in pain. The car bounced from the uneven ground, but Dakota held on, clinched her teeth, and kept driving. Before another shot, she saw her target. Helcom was dressed in a Ghillie suit and looked like part of the ground. She was on her knees with the rifle pointed up at Wilt's balloon. Dakota could see her rifle sticking out in front of the camouflaged suit.

Dakota directed her vehicle toward Helcom. The shooter was perpendicular to the direction Dakota was moving. Helcom was concentrating on sighting at the bottom of the gondola and had noise reduction earphones on, so she didn't hear or see Dakota coming until the last second. Dakota hit her going thirty miles an hour. The car bounced but Dakota didn't hear any sound. She stopped the car a few feet from the encounter, put it in reverse and once again felt the car as it ran over Helcom. She backed up far enough to see Helcom lying on the ground who was motionless. Dakota was going to get out of the car and check to see if Helcom was dead, but she heard Wilt grown. She picked up the phone and said, "Helcom has been compromised. I ran over her twice with the car. I haven't checked but I'm sure she's dead."

"You ran over her? Great thinking. You did the job sweetheart. Thank you, thank you. I have to get this balloon down now because Richard can hardly move. I've been scratched in the lower leg and took one in my butt. I'm bleeding but not incapacitated. Please call an ambulance and let them know what's going on and see if they will send on that takes two patients. I don't know where I'll land yet but I'm looking. See you on the ground."

Wilt lifted himself up to where he could see over the gondola railing. He noticed the balloon was still going up very slowly. He looked down and saw mostly dirt fields.

I could put this down anywhere below me, but it's still going up. He looked at his friend. "Richard, are you conscious enough to guide me to land this thing?"

"Yeah," he responded. "I feel like shit, but I think I can help."

"I want to put it down as quickly as possible. Dakota is calling an ambulance for us. I think you need it more than I do."

Richard struggled, and with Wilt's help, sat up on the floor with his back on the Kevlar surrounding the gondola. He looked up for a moment and told Wilt to pull on the rope that opens the top of the balloon. He indicated that would stop the accent and the balloon would start down. After that he slid over to the floor and passed out.

OK Wilt, you can do this. His leg was throbbing, and his right buttock was aching. His trousers felt wet, which Wilt knew was blood. He felt lightheaded for a moment. He shook it off and pulled on the rope Richard had pointed at. The balloon stopped rising and floated along for a moment. Once it started down it gained speed. Wilt was shocked that it started down so quickly. He knew unless he slowed it down it would hit the ground too hard. He ignored the pain and stood up and activated both burners for five seconds. The balloon slowed but was still descending too fast. Wilt activated the burners another five seconds. Still too fast. He pulled the burner ropes again, another five seconds. The balloon finally slowed as Wilt look down to see how close he was to the ground. He was shocked that the ground was only twenty feet below. He jerked the burner ropes again and the balloon showed but not enough and it hit the ground hard and tipped the gondola over. Both Richard and Wilt rolled out on the ground. Fortunately the crew was anticipating this landing and were there to grab the ropes and held the balloon in place. Dakota rolled up, jumped out of the car and ran to Wilt.

"The ambulance is right behind me. Are you OK? Please talk to me!"

"I'm a shitty balloon pilot," said Wilt. "I'm hurting but I'll make it."

"I'm going to put you in the ambulance then go back and see about Helcom. I'll see you at the hospital a little later."

The ambulance arrived and the EMT's jumped out and took over. They put Richard in the back and started an IV in his arm.

The ambulance was equipped to take two patients. Wilt was placed beside Richard and once the EMT found he was shot in the butt, they put him on his side. They were still working on the two men when Dakota decided to put Wilt's gun in the trunk of her car and drive back to determine the situation with Helcom.

CHAPTER TWENTY-FIVE

Dakota drove to where she ran over Helcom. She had a difficult time locating the area because all the dirt fields looked alike. She finally saw her tracks where she turned off the road and followed them to where she hit Helcom. Helcom wasn't there! Somehow she survived the hits.

Dakota got out of the car and surveyed the area. She could see where Helcom had crawled away because there was an indentation in the dirt, plus a blood trail. Dakota started to follow the trail, then stopped and looked around to see if the rifle was gone. She could not find it.

She took the rifle with her. How could she survive the hits? Then crawl away taking the rifle with her. She could not have gone far.

Dakota reentered her vehicle and followed the blood trail. Two hundred yards later she saw a Helcom lying in the dirt not moving. *She's losing strength.* Dakota stopped her SUV and started walking toward the wounded shooter. Helcom groaned as she turned over on her back, and slowly brought up her rifle and tried to aim it at Dakota.

Dakota stopped for a moment. I don't *think she's got the strength to pull the trigger.* As she walked forward Helcom the rifle fired. The noise startled Dakota and she jumped, but the bullet missed. She took a deep breath, Helcom's action pissed her off. She walked up and kicked the rifle out of the shooter's hands.

"If you want to live, asshole, you better start co-operating,"

Helcom closed her eyes and had trouble breathing.

Dakota stood there looking down at the shooter. *This woman, lying in front of me with her Ghillie suit on, tried to kill someone I love. I could get in the SUV and run her over a few times to ensure she was dead. Who would know? Who would blame me if I told them she wanted to shoot me. Hell, the rifle is right next to her. It would be easy. Can I do it? Should I do it?*

Helcom must have read Dakota's thoughts as she said with a whisper, "Help me, please."

Dakota pulled out her phone and called for an ambulance. "OK, hang on. I just called for an ambulance and told them where we're located, and they could see us from the road. They should be here in a little while."

With slow difficult moves Helcom pulled out a piece of paper from one of her pockets. "Please have this published for me."

Dakota read the paragraph that explained why women should be snipers. She stood looking at it and suddenly ripped in into pieces and put it in her pocket.

Dakota looked at Helcom and her labored breathing. "Try to live so you can spend the rest of your life in jail. Too bad New Mexico doesn't have the death penalty as you would be a perfect criminal for it."

Once again Helcom gathered her strength and whispered, "Each one deserved to die because they were no good. I proved I was qualified as a sniper."

"The only thing you proved was that you are a murderer. You had no right to kill those people. You had no right to judge them. If anything, you may have set back the possibility of women getting into sniper's school with your reckless and indiscriminate killings," Dakota said as her face became red with anger.

Dakota walked back to her truck, got into it and waited for the ambulance. She was looking at Helcom lying in front of her still thinking how easy it would be to run over her a few more times, but she didn't move.

* * *

Once Dakota was back in the hospital and having checked on Wilt, she called Frank Courts.

"What the hell do you mean Wilt got a personal clue about the next shooting."

"Just what I said. He knew Helcom wanted a dual to prove she was the better shooter. Problem was Wilt thought she would be in a balloon like he was, but she stayed on the ground and shot through the bottom. He's wounded twice but will be OK, and the pilot friend was hit in the shoulder and he's recovering also."

"What about the shooter?" Frank asked.

"She was run over by a car and is in the hospital. Right now, it's touch and go. She may make it, and she may not."

"Who ran her over?" asked Frank.

"I did," said Dakota. "Wilt could not see her from the balloon and wanted me to help him out. The only weapon I had was a car, so I used it."

"OK, I want a full report on my desk in a couple of days. This whole situation is really crazy."

"I agree, but the Vindictive Sniper is done."

Dakota was sitting in the waiting area while the nurse wheeled Wilt back to his room after they sewed him up. They didn't find any bullet in him and deduced both areas were only flesh wounds. Dakota heard a voice and looked up and saw that Georgie was standing looking at her.

"Georgie, how did you know about this?"

"Frank Courts called me, and I wanted to come to the hospital and see Wilt."

"Well, you can't see him yet, they just brought him out of surgery."

"Will he be OK?" she asked.

"Yes, full recovery. Just a matter of time."

"What happened to your arm?"

"The Vindictive Sniper shot me a couple of weeks ago. I'll be fine."

Georgie stood for a moment, then said, "I understand the shooter is here. What's her name?"

"Helcom Garcia."

"What room is she in?"

"She's in room three zero six. They are waiting for a bed to open up in I C U. No one can see her except a relative and I don't think any of them are here yet," said Dakota.

"Thanks," said Georgie. "I'm going to take a walk" and she left.

Dakota was outlining her report to Frank when Georgie walked back to where she was sitting.

"Is Wilt awake yet?" she asked.

"No. It may be a while yet."

"I can't wait so please tell Wilt I stopped by, will you?"

"I will, Georgie," Dakota said.

`I just had a conversation with Helcom," said Georgie. "And she said she would never shoot at Wilt again. So, Wilt is safe."

"I thought she was unconscious?" said Dakota.

"She came to just as I came into her room." Responded Georgie.

"How did you get into her room?"

"I told the nurse I was her mother. Anyway, I wish you and Wilt a long and happy life. Take care of him, OK?" she turned and walked out of the room.

A few minutes later a nurse came rushing to the waiting room. She looked at Dakota and said, "I'm looking for Helcom's mother."

Dakota didn't know what to say, "Uh, she left a little while ago, why?"

"Her daughter just passed away. I met her mother and took a break and when I came back Helcom was not breathing. Really too bad. Her mother should know. Do you know how to get a hold of her?"

"Afraid not," said Dakota.

"Damn," said the nurse and walked back down the hall.

End

ACKNOWLEDGEMENTS

My thanks go to Judy and Mike Manginella who reviewed the book and suggested many positive changes. Also, thanks to my deceased wife who reviewed the first part of the book while she was alive and contributed some good ideas.

Several of the ideas in this story came from my younger son Clay Blair. We would discuss the ideas and he would suggest changes, which I appreciate and hank him.

OTHER BOOKS PUBLISHED BY THE AUTHOR

Don't Be A Dead Fish

Last Walk at Russell Cove

Stalking the Butterfly

Murder at Mountain View, a Novella

The Turquoise Murders

ABOUT THE AUTHOR

Howard Blair has a degree in Psychology from the University of California at Davis. He was an Infantry Officer in the U. S. Marine Corps and worked for Caterpillar and Caterpillar Dealers for forty years. He has two sons and eight grandchildren. He is a member of several historical societies including Sons of the American Revolution and Sons of the Republic of Texas. He has traveled extensively and been in forty-one countries and all fifty states. He lives in Albuquerque, New Mexico.